PUMPKIN SPICE & EVERYTHING NICE

T0316072

PUMPKIN SPICE & EVERYTHING NICE

Katie Cicatelli-Kuc

SCHOLASTIC

Published in the UK by Scholastic, 2024
Scholastic, Bosworth Avenue, Warwick, CV34 6UQ
Scholastic Ireland, 89E Lagan Road, Dublin Industrial Estate, Glasnevin, Dublin, D11 HP5F

SCHOLASTIC and associated logos are trademarks and/or
registered trademarks of Scholastic Inc.

Text © Katie Cicatelli-Kuc, 2024
Book design by Stephanie Yang

ISBN 978 0702 33874 8

A CIP catalogue record for this book is available from the British Library.

Printed in UK
Paper made from wood grown in sustainable forests and other controlled sources.

MIX
Paper | Supporting
responsible forestry
FSC® C018072

3 5 7 9 10 8 6 4 2

www.scholastic.co.uk

For safety or quality concerns:
UK: www.scholastic.co.uk/productinformation
EU: www.scholastic.ie/productinformation

TO JEN, KATIE, AND DR. WANG, FOR
TELLING ME THAT I COULD, AND TO
GREG, ERIN, MOM, MILA, AND NICK,
FOR MAKING SURE THAT I DID.

1

Sometimes I feel like my hometown of Briar Glen is just showing off. I can't tear my eyes away from a brilliant maple tree right outside my classroom window. All week I've been watching its leaves slowly change from light green to orange and red, glowing against the backdrop of a mountain in the late-afternoon sun. I inhale deeply, and I swear I can almost smell the fall breeze, the crisp scent of a nearby bonfire, even from inside this stuffy room.

"Lucy? You okay?" my teacher Mrs. Ryan asks me. "You're breathing kind of hard."

I snap out of my daydream and look around the room. Everyone in my sophomore English class is looking at me—including the new guy, Jack Harper. He just moved to Briar Glen, and he has been the single topic of conversation around school. As I take in his features, I'm still not convinced he's actually a person and not a robot. People like him don't exist in real life. His eyes are green, but like the green in a crayon box green. Not hazel. Not greenish. Pure, one-hundred-percent green. And even a brick wall would notice the muscles in his arms. Yeah, no, he's not real. Definitely some kind of robot.

But then he smiles at me, and I don't think robots can smile like him. Robots shouldn't make me blush, right?

I quickly turn back to Mrs. Ryan. "Yep!"

Mrs. Ryan looks at me a second longer, unconvinced. "Okay," she finally says, "*Great Expectations*! Who wants to tell me why they think Pip is ashamed of Joe?"

I dig through my backpack, trying to find my paperback copy of *Great Expectations*. Maybe if I look busy, Mrs. Ryan won't call on me, because I might have sorta fallen asleep during the assigned reading last night. But where is my book? I know I put it in here somewh—Aha! There it is, under my history book. I try to pull *Great Expectations* out, but it's stuck on something. What the heck is in my bag? I give the paperback a big tug and then—

Riiip!

Sigh. Of course. I hold *Great Expectations* in my hand, sans cover, and look up.

Mrs. Ryan clears her throat, an eyebrow raised. "You sure, Lucy?"

Everyone is staring at me. Again. Including Jack Harper.

This time I glance at Melanie Craddock, who sits right next to

Jack. The head of the cheerleading squad. Could they be a more cliché good-looking couple? Not that they are a couple yet. They definitely will be by Halloween, though. At the latest.

Melanie leans forward in her desk and says something to Jack, flashing her million-kilowatt smile, then flips her long brown curly hair over her shoulder.

"All good!" I say to Mrs. Ryan, turning back to face her, still holding my torn book. I listen as everyone talks about Pip's shame.

Toward the end of class, I turn to look at the clock and . . . it almost seems like Jack is staring at me? Weird. Must be some kind of programming error.

Finally—*finally*—the bell rings, and I hop out of my seat. It's three o'clock, which means I need to get to my mom's coffee shop, Cup o' Jo, like, *now*. It's a Friday afternoon in October, and I know she's slammed with leaf-peeping tourists.

I head to my locker, where one of my best friends, Evie, is waiting for me. "I knew you weren't a huge Dickens fan, but wow, a bit dramatic?" she says, looking at the coverless book in my hand.

"It got stuck on something. The cover ripped. Like, in the middle of class. Which was apparently hilarious to everyone, including Jack—"

"Harper, who is heading this way!"

"Huh?" I start to turn but in my haste, I somehow manage to tip over my bag, spilling its contents everywhere. Great. I bend down, trying to shovel everything back in it.

Evie kneels to help me. "Not to alarm you or anything," she whispers, "but he's, like, two feet away."

"What?"

"Hey, uh, Lucy?" I hear a voice behind me say.

I look at Evie, who smirks. She stands up first and I follow, turn, and . . . Jack Harper is standing right in front of me.

I've only ever seen him from across the classroom, and this close up, I realize how much taller he is than me (I barely clock in at five feet two). He has freckles across his nose and cheeks. And I can see that his eyes are even more sparkly, and wow, his eyelashes really are long . . .

I also realize he has just asked me something, but I have no idea what. "Sorry, what did you say?"

He registers my confusion. "I said, I know, it's weird, but . . . I have copies of a few different editions of *Great Expectations*. It's my favorite Dickens novel."

"That's . . . cool," I say, my brain short-circuiting. Why is he telling me this?

"Do you want one of my copies?" he asks, as if he can read my mind. "Without a ripped cover?"

"Oh, right. Thanks, that's . . . nice of you," I say, finally understanding why Jack Harper is standing at my locker, talking to me.

"How, uh, how are you liking it so far?" he asks.

"The book is . . . fine. Still readable. Or apparently readable."

"She hates Dickens," Evie says. I'd almost forgotten she was there.

"Hates Dickens?!" Jack mimes stabbing himself in the heart. "You can't hate *all* Dickens. What about *A Tale of Two Cities*?"

"It cured her insomnia," Evie says brightly.

"Evie!" I say, feeling my face flush.

"Just drive that dagger in farther!" Jack says, his hand on his chest.

"Um, sorry," I say. "I mean, thanks. I'm cool with the book I have. But if I change my mind . . . I'll let you know?"

Jack sighs. "How can you not like *Great Expectations*?" He looks at Evie as if she'll have an answer, but she just shrugs.

"Different strokes?" Evie suggests.

"Fair enough." Jack laughs. "See you later."

"You too!" I say.

For a moment, Jack gives me a confused look, and then he's on his way down the hall.

It's not until he's on the staircase leading outside that I realize what I said to Jack Harper makes no sense. But it's okay because Jack Harper makes no sense to me.

"'You too'?" Evie says, looking at me, one eyebrow raised.

"I'm in a hurry!"

"Uh-huh," Evie says. "So he's cute and he likes to read. And he just offered to give you one of his books and you said no. I think that's, like, a cardinal sin, to turn down a book when a book nerd offers you one."

"He's not a book nerd!" I say. "He was just being nice."

"Uh-huh," Evie repeats.

"I think you're just jealous that you're not the newest kid at school anymore." It had been a bit of a running joke between Evie, me, and our other best friend, Amber. Even though Evie moved to Briar Glen two years ago, in eighth grade, we still call her the new kid.

"I'm green with envy," she says sarcastically.

I roll my eyes, then check the time on my phone. "Oh man, I really gotta go."

"Yeah, don't want your boss to fire you," Evie teases. She pulls a compact out of her pocket, examining her cat's-eye eyeliner. "I need to fix this," she says with a sigh, then turns in the direction of the bathrooms. "See you this weekend!"

I close my bag, pick up my pace, and head out of the building. But I don't get far before I hear—

"Lucy!" Amber says, jogging over to me from the soccer fields. "We have to run a million laps today at practice for no reason. I'm warming up," she says, impatiently swatting her long blond ponytail away from her head.

"Poor Amber," I say. "It must be hard to be such a soccer star."

Amber squints her brown eyes at me. She's on the varsity team even though she's only a sophomore. "Seriously! You try running all those laps! I'm going to get shin splints."

"No thanks!" I say brightly. Amber and I have a lot in common—a shared addiction to competitive cooking and baking TV shows, a severe dislike of the color beige—but athleticism is not one of them.

"I'll stop by the shop tomorrow? Save me a corner Rice Krispies treat?"

"Always," I promise. With a smile and a nod, Amber heads back to the soccer fields.

It's a ten-minute walk to Main Street. A walk I can do in eight minutes when I'm in a hurry, like I usually am. My mom has a handful of part-time workers, but I still want to get to the shop as quickly as I can to relieve her of some of the craziness.

I pull my dirty blond hair up in a messy bun as I walk quickly down the quiet, treelined streets, which are a mixture of colonial and craftsman style and even a few Victorian houses. Paper cutout pumpkins, ghosts, and spiders fill the windows, and pumpkins, jack-o'-lanterns, and gourds of all shapes and sizes adorn the porches. I pause for just a second outside my favorite Halloween house: the one with the huge pirate ship with a literal skeleton crew. There is some sort of human-size sea monster with long tentacles at the helm of the boat. Every year on Halloween night, the sea monster actually steers the ship, and it's been a debate among Briar Glen residents whether there is someone inside the sea monster costume or if it's operating through animatronics. Something about the way the monster looks at me through those beady eyes every Halloween . . . I shiver and move on.

I round the corner onto Main Street, and as usual at this time of year, it's bustling with tourists. People milling around in our brick brownstone local artisanal shops and galleries. People taking selfies and pictures of one another on the narrow sidewalk, oblivious to me or really anything other than the foliage surrounding them. I can't blame the tourists, though. The leaves are on fire with color, the sun is lighting up the mountain, and there's a crisp fall breeze gently blowing down Main Street.

As I try to squeeze past one group slowly strolling on the sidewalk and attempting to take a selfie, a woman turns to me. "Oh, I'm so sorry!" she says. "We're totally blocking the sidewalk, aren't we? It's just so—"

"Beautiful." I smile. "I know. It's okay. I live here, and fall still amazes me every year."

"You get to live here! Lucky girl."

I look at the glowing mountain again, the vibrant leaves dancing in the wind. "Yeah, I am."

The group follows my gaze and gasps. They ready themselves for another selfie.

"Enjoy your visit to Briar Glen," I say, but they don't hear me—and it's okay. The mountain and the multi-hued leaves speak for themselves. My words would never be enough to describe Briar Glen in the fall.

I take a step in the street to go around the group, then hop back onto the sidewalk. I'm about to cross the street to my mom's coffee shop, but I take a quick look behind me at the empty storefront, which was a florist shop for as long as I can remember. I'm not really a flower kind of person, but I still used to love watching Jen make arrangements, listening to the stories she'd tell me about bride- and groomzillas. The shop has been empty since spring, when Jen decided to retire and move down south somewhere. I think South Carolina? I can never remember where exactly. I don't know why anyone would ever move away from Briar Glen. I can't imagine living anywhere else.

Everyone has been guessing what'll go in the space. My

favorite guess was Lucky's, the town barber: a Froyo place where you can add as many toppings as you want.

But as I look at the empty storefront again, I notice a flier taped to the inside of the door. That wasn't there yesterday. I can't see what it says, so I get closer.

SEE YOU SOON! EVERYONE'S FAVORITE COFFEE SHOP WILL BE HERE SHORTLY!

And then I gasp.

Underneath the words is a logo for one of the most popular coffee chains in the world: Java Junction.

Which is opening across the street from our coffee shop.

2

I stare at the sign, glued to the spot, the Java Junction logo burning into my eyes. I look around at the crowded sidewalks, then across the street at Cup o' Jo. Even this late in the afternoon, after three o'clock, people are still going into the shop. My mom's adorable coffee shop! Her shop: as in she started the business herself, runs it herself. Has run it herself since I was little. I started helping her out here and there when I was thirteen, but now that I'm sixteen I'm working with her almost every day after school and most weekends. She's got a couple other employees, Sheva and Danielle, and a few backup part-time employees, but she still brews all the coffee, crafts all our drinks, creates all our pastries, and often bakes, too. You name it, she does it.

Generic Java Junction won't last a week in Briar Glen.

When I turn back to look at the sign, two tourists are peering at it. "Ooh, Java Junction is coming here!" the man says to his female friend.

"I bet the Java Junction pumpkin spice latte tastes even better in Briar Glen," the woman says.

"Oh, totally!" the man says.

They continue on their way, but I glare at their retreating figures. Do they realize that Java Junction pumpkin spice lattes are chemically laden mass-produced drinks that don't contain an ounce of real pumpkin?!

Even so, as I watch them pose for a selfie in front of another amber-leaved tree, a small, cold worry tugs at my stomach.

But I quickly shake my head. I'm sure it'll be fine. Cup o' Jo has such a loyal customer base, and tourists fill our shop every weekend. Java Junction doesn't stand a chance here. It'll be totally fine. Right?

I look across the street at Cup o' Jo again and realize I don't have any more time to think about Java Junction or pumpkin spice lattes because I need to get to work at my mom's coffee shop, which is way better than any silly coffee chain. Java Junction is going to regret ever setting foot in Briar Glen!

I cross the street and push open Cup o' Jo's door, the bell jingling. Joni Mitchell is softly playing over the small speakers we installed in the walls. I inhale the smell of freshly brewed coffee and coffee beans. It sounds and smells like home.

My mom pops up from behind the pastry display case, holding

an empty tray. "Lucy! The carrot cake muffins were a huge success!" she says proudly. "Maybe a good contender for the fall festival?"

"Maybe!" I say, and grin as I walk behind the counter and pull my work apron on. The muffins were something I thought of, and together she and I created the perfect recipe. Crafting recipes and testing them is my favorite part of helping my mom at the shop. And it often inspires me to think of the perfect dessert for the fall festival's baking competition.

But I look at my mom more closely as she scrubs the tray over the sink behind the counter. Something in her expression isn't quite right. "You okay?"

It's always been just my mom and me. She wanted it that way, and I can't imagine it any other way, either. She knows me better than anyone else on the planet, and I know her better than anyone else on the planet, too. Including ourselves sometimes.

Then, duh, it hits me: I'm such an irresponsible employee! "I'm sorry I'm late," I say. "I ran into someone on my way out of school, and he wanted me to borrow his book, and I think he's a robot."

My mom laughs. "What are you talking about?"

"Nothing," I say impatiently. "Just the new guy, Jack Harper. That's who I was talking to. He's, like, so stereotypically good-looking and nice, it's annoying. And apparently he loves literature.

I don't think he's an actual person. I think he's a robot." I move my arms robotically. "It's his fault I am late," I say in a robot voice.

My mom laughs again, but something about her laugh is off now, too. "I don't even know what time it is," she says. "Are you late?"

I sneak a look at my phone. "Uh, yeah. I mean, no!"

She doesn't say anything, just stares out the front window. "Did you see the Java Junction sign?" she finally asks.

"Yeah," I say slowly, hesitantly.

I wait for her to say more, but she doesn't.

"Is this something we need to be worried about?" I cautiously ask.

"Worried?" She looks thoughtful, considering the question. "We're busy every weekend, every afternoon. Why would people travel to Briar Glen and get coffee at some place they could get coffee from anywhere?"

Her confident words should make me feel a little better. But she's not looking at me as she talks, and that cold thing is still tugging at my stomach. I smile and say, "Yeah, good points."

I look around our shop, trying to see it through fresh eyes. Before it was Cup o' Jo, the building used to be a house that belonged to the Blackwell family, some sort of second cousins of my mom's, for generations. The last Blackwell, Dorothy, never had kids, so the building became my mom's.

I look around at the people here, like Devon Stern, a college student who used to babysit me, who is tapping away at her laptop at one of the handful of tables we have scattered throughout the shop. Others, like Sarah Jay, a woman my mom went to college with and a freelance event planner, are sitting on stools by the windows at the front, looking out at Briar Glen. One corner of the shop has a couple of mismatched vintage armchairs next to a bookshelf. It's become a free book library over the years, and right now it's scattered with paperbacks, children's picture books, and even cookbooks.

All way cuter, cozier, and overall *better* than cookie-cutter Java Junction.

I want to point this all out to my mom, and talk to her more, but a customer walks in. Someone I don't recognize, so they must be a tourist.

"Hello!" I say in my cheeriest voice. "What would you like today?"

He orders one of our most popular drinks, a maple latte, a drink I could make in my sleep. I pour our custom-made maple syrup blend into a coffee mug, brew the espresso, and steam the milk. I add the espresso to the mug, then the milk. I give it a quick froth, top the drink with whipped cream and a dash of cinnamon, and hand it to the man. He takes an appreciative sip of the drink and says, "This is the best latte I've ever had," wiping whipped cream off his nose.

"Thanks!" I'm not surprised to hear him say it, but the praise always feels good. "Have a lovely day."

After him, a group of three tourists walks in. They all order iced coffees, one with oat milk, another with soy milk, and the third, black. As I ring them up, one of them takes a picture of her coffee, and the second peers into the pastry case.

But then the third woman says, "You don't have pumpkin spice lattes here?"

I feel my customer service smile fade from my face for just a second. "No, sorry, we don't. We don't use any artificial ingredients here, and pumpkin spice lattes are full of them. Did you know that pumpkin spice lattes don't even contain an ounce of real pumpkin? Not a single ounce!"

The woman frowns a bit, but the one looking into the pastry case says, "We could always hit up Java Junction later."

"Oh, true," the first woman, Oat Milk Iced Coffee, says.

"It's not open yet," I sputter, trying to keep the panic out of my voice.

"That's too bad," Oat Milk says, her voice flat.

"Is it?" I say before I can stop myself. "I mean, thanks for stopping by! Enjoy your drinks!"

"Have a nice day!" they say together, then leave the shop, their phones out, taking more pictures of their drinks.

I'm rattled after they leave. I don't like being rattled.

My mom joins me at the register. "What did they order?" she asks. It's a question she used to ask me early on in my Cup o' Jo days, back when she wanted to track what our most popular drinks were, so I'm surprised she's asking me now.

I scowl. "Iced coffees. One of them wanted a stupid pumpkin spice latte."

My mom is quiet for a second.

"What?" I say impatiently. "What are you thinking about?"

"Listen, I know your feelings about pumpkin spice lattes—"

"Yeah, the complete nausea they induce, you mean?" I interrupt.

"Lucy," she says warningly.

"Mom, there could not be a more clichéd and artificially sweet and gross drink. There isn't even—"

"An ounce of real pumpkin in a pumpkin spice latte," my mom interrupts. "I know." She sighs. "I just think we need to keep our options open."

"What do you mean, 'our options'?" I ask.

"It's just . . . with Java Junction going in across the street, we're going to have some competition."

"I thought you said we don't need to be worried, that we have a loyal customer base?" I say, the cold thing in my stomach coming back again.

"We do," my mom says quickly. "But we want to keep it that way. And part of that may be expanding our menu a bit."

"Please tell me this is a joke," I groan. "Someone is setting me up, right?"

My mom gives me an evil grin. "Did I trick you?"

And for a second I almost believe her, that this is all a joke, that one of the world's biggest coffee chains isn't really opening up across the street from our little coffee shop. But then I see the worried look on her face, and I realize there is nothing funny about this situation at all.

"I'll think about it," I finally say. "Strongly think about it."

"Good girl," my mom says, giving me a hug.

"Good mom," I say, hugging her back. One of our many silly inside jokes. I can't even remember when it started or who started it. Sometimes with my mom it's hard to know where she begins and where I end.

3

I wake up at five the next morning. Our purple Victorian house is quiet—even Pancakes the cat is still asleep while my mom and I get ready. By the front door, she pulls on her chunky gray cardigan she's had for as long as I can remember.

I grab a hoodie, but my mom says, "It's chilly this morning. How about a jacket?"

"Yes, Mom," I say, grabbing my army-green jacket from the closet.

"Don't 'yes, Mom' me!" she says, but she's smiling as she pulls on her fingerless gloves.

Once we're outside, I'm glad I took her advice. It's a chilly morning, and foggy, too, which makes it feel even cooler. I can barely see the mountain on our five-minute walk to the shop.

When we get to Cup o' Jo, I start making two pecan pies. The pie crusts chilled overnight in the fridge, so I pop them in the oven. While the crusts are baking, I cream butter in the mixer, then add honey and syrup. Next is vanilla, nutmeg, and salt. I crack the eggs into the mixture, one at a time. I've just finished putting the pecans in the pie shells and am about to add the filling when Sheva and Danielle arrive. Before I know it, the pies are baked, and it's seven, and there is a small line of people waiting to get in.

My mom looks at me, unlocks the door, and says, "Ready?"

"Ready," I say, and smile.

This small conversation has been our ritual since I started helping her at the coffee shop, but yeah, okay, it still gives me goose bumps.

And then, we're officially open.

The morning passes quickly, as most fall Saturdays do. I see faces I've known my entire life: neighbors, other Main Street shop owners, my mom's friends, classmates' parents, a teacher here and there. And I also see about a million faces I don't recognize: tourists here for the day, the weekend, sometimes even the week. I think it's pretty cool that I live in such a beautiful place that people travel here from all over the country, and sometimes even all over the world, to visit.

Around mid-morning, the door opens, and another one of our regulars, my middle school geography teacher, Mrs. Vervone, walks in.

"Good morning, ladies," she says as my mom starts to make her maple latte.

"Morning," I say.

"You know, Java Junction has some nerve, opening up across the street from you guys," Mrs. Vervone says as I ring her up.

My mom smiles tightly and hands over Mrs. Vervone's coffee. "Why would it make a difference that they're opening across the street from us?" she says.

Mrs. Vervone frowns. "Because they're the biggest coffee chain in the world?"

"*One* of the biggest coffee chains," I quickly interject. "And besides, why come to Briar Glen just to go to a coffee shop you can go to anywhere, right?" I say, winking at my mom.

"Well," Mrs. Vervone says, "you'll never see me set foot inside that place!"

"That's sweet," my mom says. "We appreciate your loyalty, Jane! But really, it's no big deal!" She smiles, but I see a weird new line on her forehead. A worry line.

Mrs. Vervone looks skeptical. "I think it's incredibly disrespectful to open so close to a Briar Glen institution!"

I agree with her, but after looking at my mom again, I decide to keep my mouth shut.

My mom simply smiles and says, "Enjoy this beautiful weekend!"

Mrs. Vervone finally stops frowning. "You too! Don't let Java Junction get you down!" she says before she walks out the door.

Just before lunch, Amber comes in. I pull out the oversized corner Rice Krispies treat I've been saving for her. One of these days I'll convince her that corner pieces of any dessert are far inferior to the middle pieces.

"You are the best, Lucy," she says, ripping the plastic wrap off and taking a huge bite of the treat.

"Oh, I know!"

"Hey . . . did you . . . see what's going in across the street?"

"Yep!" I say through gritted teeth.

She looks at me, surprised. "You and your mom aren't worried or anything, are you?"

I feel my face heating up. "Why would we be worried about one of the world's biggest coffee chains going in across the street from my mom's coffee shop? What could possibly go wrong?" I laugh, somewhat maniacally.

"What's so funny?" my mom asks, coming back from the fridge, her arms full of milk containers.

"Nothing!" Amber and I say at the same time.

"Wow, that's totally believable," my mom says. Amber and I have been best friends since kindergarten, and if we were into it,

Amber would totally call my mom Aunt Jo. But our family isn't into it, and neither is Amber, really. But she *could* call my mom Aunt Jo, and I *could* call her moms Aunt Laura and Aunt Nico.

"What's up, girls?" my mom says as she pours milk into pitchers.

When neither one of us answers her, she looks at us expectantly. "What is it?" she asks a little more sharply.

"Amber was just asking what we thought about Java Junction," I say casually.

My mom frowns. "And?"

"And I was just saying that they don't stand a chance against you guys!" Amber says awkwardly.

"A chance against us for what?" my mom asks.

"Nothing!" Amber says.

My mom's frown deepens.

Amber sighs. "I mean, elephant in the room, but Java Junction is a huge coffee chain and—"

"And I already told Lucy there is nothing to worry about!" my mom says tightly. "We have a loyal customer base, and we're busy with tourists every weekend. And like I also already told Lucy, why would people make the trip to Briar Glen just to go to a coffee shop they could go to anywhere? Now that's the last I want to talk about it. With either of you!"

She smiles, but I notice the new worry line on her forehead again. It reminds me of the cold thing I felt in my stomach yesterday, but I decide to ignore it.

Amber smiles back. "You got it, boss."

"Ew, why are you calling me boss?" my mom says.

We all laugh, and again, the worry about Java Junction fades from my mind.

The rest of the day passes slowly. Quietly. I'm not sure why, but the silence between my mom and me feels a little strained. Maybe it's just my imagination, though.

Some more regulars come in, some tourists, too. Some people talk about Java Junction. Most don't.

But then, just before closing, three tourists walk in.

I greet them with a friendly "Hello, how can I help you?"

Two of them order iced coffees, but the third, a woman about my mom's age, bites her lip. "Do you have pumpkin spice lattes?"

I feel my smile turn into a grimace but say, "We don't serve pumpkin spice lattes here."

The woman stares at me blankly for a second, and then says, "Oh. That's weird. Too bad that Java Junction across the street isn't open yet. Pumpkin spice lattes are, like, their livelihood."

My mom is next to me, preparing another drink, and gives

me a look. Then she says, "I actually just made a fresh batch of pumpkin spice this morning!"

I look back at her—the traitor!—but I say to the customer, "I'd be happy to make you a pumpkin spice latte, then!" The words hurt to say.

"Oh, okay, that'd be great!" the woman says.

"Great!" I say, matching her tone with fake enthusiasm.

The woman stares at me expectantly, so I get to work. Despite how annoying I find the drink, it's not very hard to make. Especially since my mom apparently just made a fresh batch of pumpkin spice. And especially since it doesn't contain any real pumpkin. Which *is* pretty gross when I think about it. But unlike Java Junction, we use real, actual spices, not chemicals, to make our lattes.

While the milk heats, I brew the espresso and pour it into a cup. I add a splash of maple syrup, our homemade spice mix, and a dash of vanilla. Then I froth the milk and pour it into the cup. I add some whipped cream and sprinkle some cinnamon on top for a final touch. Despite myself, I do have to admit that it looks like a good drink.

I slide the drink over to the woman. "Enjoy!"

My mom rings up the order and says, "You're in for a treat!" She smiles at me, and I try to smile back.

The woman claps and squeals. "This looks amazing! Thank you!" She picks up the drink and takes a small sip. She closes her eyes. "What a pumpkin spice latte!"

It pains me a bit to see her enjoy a drink I dislike, but then I look at my mom, and the relief on her face is almost worth my discomfort. (Okay, it's totally worth my discomfort.)

As we watch the women leave the shop, my mom says, "Good girl."

"Good mom," I say, putting my arm around her.

4

The next morning, Sunday, my mom and I are up at five again. When we get to the shop, I decide to bake an apple crisp, using apples from an orchard only a few miles away from Briar Glen. As I peel the apples, my mind wanders to the festival baking competition again. Maybe some sort of apple crumb cake? While the crisp bakes, I start looking up recipes on my phone. I find a video of an influencer on social media making an apple cake that I think would do well. Soon, though, the crisp is done, and it's time to open the shop.

We're busy all morning—so busy that none of us has time to restock supplies, until finally, just before lunch, we're out of all our coffee creamers. I tell my mom and Danielle that I'll be right back and head to the storage area, where our refrigerator is. I'm still thinking about the fall festival baking competition as I refill the pitchers. I've got them cradled in my arms, and I close the fridge door with my hip.

Apple upside-down cake? I wonder as I turn around. And then I almost drop all the pitchers.

Because standing at the front of Cup o' Jo, studying the menu, is Jack Harper.

Jack Harper is here. As in *here*, here. As in here in my coffee shop. Standing about twenty feet away from me. My mom is talking to him, and he's talking back, and I try to force myself to move, but my legs seem to be made of cement and the walk takes forever.

My mom turns as I approach, and Jack turns to see what she's looking at. And she's looking at me. So now he's looking at me.

"Oh hey, Lucy," he says. "I didn't know you worked here." His eyes are doing that twinkly sparkly thing again, and he's smiling, and did his voice get even hotter?

I shake my head. I am at work. I am a professional. "Hey, Jack," I say, trying to keep my voice level.

My mom says, "I'm going to go grab some more napkins, okay, Lucy?"

She gives me a knowing grin, which I refuse to return, because there is nothing to know. Except that Jack Harper is in our shop.

I look at the line of customers behind him, and Sheva says, "I can take orders over here!" She also gives me a grin that I'd classify as knowing, but again I refuse to return it.

I turn back to Jack. "My mom owns Cup o' Jo," I say as she walks away, unable to keep the pride out of my voice.

He raises an eyebrow. "Whoa, that's cool."

"Yep, she's owned it since I was a kid. Running it, making drinks, baking, working here, keeping track of sales, pretty much everything. Yes, I know I am totally dorking out about my mom, so you don't need to tell me."

He laughs, and I realize it's the first time I've heard the sound. Something about it is so innocent, so boyish sounding. It's annoyingly cute. "That's awesome, Lucy," he says, and somehow I know he genuinely means it.

"Thanks. I mean, yeah. I mean, what would you like?" Why am I flustered?

He laughs that annoyingly cute laugh again. "Hmm, well, it is fall, so how about something autumnal?"

"What word did you just say?"

"Autumnal?"

"I've never heard that word in my life."

"You live in the most quintessential fall town ever and work in a coffee shop that I'm assuming serves autumnal beverages and you don't know the word *autumnal*?"

"Well, I do now," I say impatiently. "Though I'm still not convinced you didn't just make it up."

He laughs again—why does his laugh sound like that?—and I can't help it, I smile back at him.

"Anyway, what sort of *autumnal* beverage would you like?"

"I'd love to have a pumpkin spice latte," he says without hesitation.

I narrow my eyes at him. "Please tell me you're joking."

"Um . . . no?" he says, looking confused. "I'd really like a pumpkin spice latte."

"Well, that's not going to happen here."

"What? You're messing with me, right? It's like the most seasonal beverage ever. It's why seasonal beverages exist in the first place!"

I put up my hands. "Whoa, whoa, whoa. That's a bit of a stretch, don't you think? The reason seasonal beverages exist, really?"

"Okay, maybe a slight exaggeration on my part, but still! Don't tell me you are trying to deny the delight of a pumpkin spice latte?"

"Did you seriously just use the word *delight*?"

"*Delight* is the perfect word!" he says defensively.

"Delightfully autumnal," I mutter.

He smirks. "Wait, you seriously don't serve pumpkin spice lattes?"

"Yes, seriously. They're not on the menu. It's just so . . . overdone.

We're more creative than that. And do you know how many chemicals go into most of them? And that many pumpkin spice lattes or pumpkin-flavored anything don't contain even an ounce of real, actual pumpkin?"

He puts his hands up. "You've made your point. No delightfully autumnal pumpkin spice latte for me, I get it."

I smile a bit, but quickly fold my arms across my chest, still trying to reconcile with the fact that Jack Harper likes pumpkin spice lattes.

"I'll take one of . . ." He looks around at the display case of pastries and desserts. "One of these. A slice," he says, pointing to the pecan pie.

"Good choice." I cut a piece of pie, put it on a plate, and slide the plate to him.

I ring up the sale at the register, but he's already digging into the pie.

Sheva's line is getting long, but she just winks at me and takes the next order.

"Holy cow, this is really good," Jack says, his mouth full.

I smile and feel myself glow with pride.

"Thanks," I say. "I've made so many of them over the years. I could probably make them with my eyes closed."

But Jack doesn't seem to be listening. He's thinking about

something. "You know, I think this is better than the mini pecan pies we sell at Java Junction."

I feel my blood pressure increase at the mention of Java Junction. But also—

"What do you mean *we*?" I ask, confused.

"We. My family."

"What does your family have to do with Java Junc—?" Suddenly, it all hits me. Everything at once. "Wait, are you telling me your family owns the Java Junction across the street?"

He grins, looking almost bashful. "Yeah, that's what I'm telling you."

"That's why you moved to Briar Glen," I say, dazed.

"That's why we moved to Briar Glen," he repeats. "We were going to open a Java Junction in Atlanta, but there are already so many there, and we wanted to be in a smaller town, something with character. Charm. So we ended up here! I thought you knew the whole story already? This town is small! It's going to take some getting used to . . ." He trails off, looking at me. "You okay?" he asks cautiously.

I am anything but okay. I am the opposite of okay. I think about how hard my mom has worked my entire life for this coffee shop. All the work she has done. All the energy and love she has put into her drinks, her food. I think about my mom's worried face. What Java Junction's opening could potentially do to our shop. Oh, I am so not okay.

Before I even know what I'm doing, I reach down into the pastry case, pick up the pecan pie, and . . .

Throw it at Jack's face.

We stand there, both of us in shocked silence. The chatter in Sheva's line of customers instantly stops, as do the voices in the rest of the shop. Even the music is quiet, between songs.

I feel many eyes on me, including Jack's, but my mouth drops open. A stranger has taken over my body, and I've lost the ability to speak. And then, to my horror, Jack Harper, who is standing in my coffee shop, is covered in pie that I threw at him.

I threw a pie at him.

At Jack Harper.

And then, to my absolute horror, he . . . starts to laugh.

And then some of the people in Sheva's line start to laugh, nervously at first, and then other people at the tables start to laugh.

Jack laughs harder, pie falling off his face in thick chunks. "Folks, she has totally nailed it!"

I look at him, confused, but he's not meeting my eye. He's bowing, more pie dripping from his face to the floor.

He stands and applauds. "Lucy, you are *so* ready for the food-fight scene in our play."

Our play?

He gives me just the quickest of winks and says, "Maybe next time we should try a pie with more whipped cream, though?"

"Right," I say, playing along. "More whipped cream."

"I didn't know you were in a play!" Sheva says to me, beaming. "You know I studied theater in college, right?"

I laugh awkwardly, and the rest of the chatter around the shop slowly picks up again. Still, though, I catch a few lingering looks from some people in Sheva's line.

I grab a fistful of napkins and hand them to Jack. "Why did you—"

"Lucy!" my mom interjects as she comes to the front of the shop.

"Mom, I can explain."

"Your daughter has an excellent arm!" Jack says. "She's a natural pie thrower, perfect for her part in the food-fight scene of the school play. Also, this pie is delicious." He scoops more pie into his mouth.

"School play?" my mom repeats. She knows I'm not in any kind of school play, but she just smiles politely at Jack, then gives a quick look around at the customers back on their laptops, back to taking pictures of their drinks.

Sheva leans over and says, "You never told me your daughter was an actor!"

"No, I suppose I never did," my mom says, but she's looking at me the whole time.

"Mom, Jack's parents own the Java Junction across the street!" I say quickly. "It's his parents' fault that Cup o' Jo is—"

"Oh! How lovely!" my mom interrupts, talking to Jack. "I'll have to come over and introduce myself to them."

Her genuineness is almost as shocking as the pie all over Jack's face. I look at her, once again speechless. She says it lightly, almost cheerfully, like she's trying to smooth things over. As much as someone can after her daughter throws a pie at a customer's face.

Jack straightens up, his laughter settling down a bit. "This really is delicious pie." He picks up other pieces of pie from the counter, from the floor, and throws them into the trash can.

"Oh! We can do that," my mom says. She gives me a warning look, telling me this conversation is nowhere close to being over, and jogs to the back of the shop to retrieve the mop.

I help Jack scoop up sticky pieces of pie from the counter. "I'm sorry," I say as I toss a gooey handful into the trash. "You didn't have to say that thing about the school play, either."

Jack looks at me, a pecan chunk on his cheek. I resist the urge to remove it, to touch him. To my annoyance he starts laughing again.

"You know, I've lived in many places, traveled to lots of places, and done lots of things. But that is the first time someone has ever thrown a pie at me."

His laughter just makes me seethe all over again. "Well, I'm *so* glad I can help you cross things off your bucket list!" I snap back.

My mom appears with the mop. "Lucy, I'm going to clean this up. Can you get some more paper towels from the back?" She poses it as a question, but I know she's not asking me. She's telling me.

I sigh and head to the stockroom. Except the paper towels aren't where they're supposed to be. I know we have some. I saw them earlier today. I saw my mom place an order for them a few days ago. I dig around and finally find them in a box of extra mugs.

"Got them!" I say, walking quickly to the front of the shop. But the words die on my lips.

Jack is just about to walk out the door. Into the world. Suddenly, the gravity of what I've done is catching up with me. Fast. Once he sets foot out that door, he can tell anyone what I did. Everyone. If he decides to put it on social media, everyone at Briar Glen High could know within minutes that I, Lucy Kane, threw a pie in the face of our hot new guy. Annoyingly nice, on his way to becoming super popular new guy.

"Wait!" I say, in a panic.

Jack turns to me, an eyebrow raised.

I look around at the crowded shop, tourists walking in, totally unaware of what they've just missed, and hurry over to where Jack is standing.

"I'm sorry, okay," I say quickly. "For throwing the pie. It was a stupid thing to do. It's also a stupid thing for your parents to put a Java Junction across the street from Cup o' Jo . . ."

I stop myself, take a breath, glance at him, expecting him to look hurt. But he doesn't. He just looks curious.

So I go on, "I'm sorry. Really. But maybe it could be a thing that the whole school doesn't have to hear about? I know you're new here, but Briar Glen is small. So small. And, like, when people do dumb things like throw pie at people, other people talk. A lot. For a long time. Do you know how long it took for people to stop talking about Jason Morris wetting the bed on a Boy Scout trip because the ghost stories scared him so much?"

I don't give Jack a chance to answer. "A long time!" I say. "A really, really long time."

Jack smiles that easy smile, and I swear that I can see his eyes twinkle. How on earth does he do that? "Lucy, it's cool. What happens at Cup o' Jo, stays at Cup o' Jo."

I give him another pleading look.

"Lucy, seriously, don't sweat it," Jack says, apparently seeing the pure panic I'm feeling.

"How do I know I can trust you?" I sputter.

All the anger I felt at Jack and his family has been placed on a temporary shelf somewhere else in my brain because now all I'm thinking about is how Jack is going to tell everyone at school what happened, and this legacy is going to follow me for the rest of my time at Briar Glen High School, and probably well into my college years and adulthood. I'm picturing a high school reunion, all of us graying middle-aged versions of ourselves, and someone says, "Hey remember when Lucy threw that pie at Jack?"

Jack shrugs. "Because I'm giving you my word." Like it's that simple, that easy.

He walks out the door, the bell jingling, before I have a chance to say anything else.

The door closes behind him. I don't want to turn around and face my mom or her anger.

I don't need to because my mom meets me at the door. "Let's have a chat, okay?" she says, gesturing to the back of the shop, where there's an empty table.

We walk past Devon, who is now sitting with Caiming, another one of my former babysitters. I wave at them, smiling, but when I get to the back of the shop with my mom, my smile quickly fades.

"Lucy, sweetie, can you please tell me *why* you threw pie at a customer? And don't even try to tell me you're in a play, because we both know you're not."

"Mom! Don't you understand? His parents. They own the Java Junction. Hearing Jack say that name, and knowing his connection with it, and what that could mean for Cup o' Jo . . ." I trail off. "Obviously he's a jerk, and his parents must be, too."

"We don't know that—"

"Who opens a chain coffee shop across the street from a coffee shop that has been here for years?" I practically shout.

"Lucy!" my mom hisses, looking around the shop. Luckily, no one seems to be paying any attention to us. "We are going to be mature, kind business owners. We can't just go around throwing pie at people, okay?" And, then, to my surprise, my mom laughs. She actually laughs.

"You think this is funny now, too?" I sputter.

"No! Yes!" she says, and then she laughs more. "You know, I think you should take the afternoon off," she says, when she finally stops laughing. I realize that the worry line is back on her forehead.

"Am I in trouble?" I hate that I sound like I'm five years old.

"No, of course not. At least, I don't think so. But I do want you to spend some time with your friends. Why don't you go apple picking this afternoon with Evie and Amber?"

"I don't know, it'd be fun but—"

"No buts."

"Fine," I grumble.

"Go outside and enjoy the fresh air, okay? Just stay away from any pies." She winks.

"Very funny," I say, but the mention of the word *pie* makes me wonder again who Jack has told about what I've done.

I wait outside, buttoning up my jacket, inhaling the fresh fall air. I smell a bonfire somewhere, too. I look anywhere but at the Java Junction storefront.

Soon, Laura and Nico pull up in their car. Amber is in the back seat. "You're free!" she jokes as I pull my seat belt on. She sees my face, though, and says, "What's up? Is everything okay?"

I take a deep breath. "Yes, everything is fine. Sort of fine?" I pause, unsure how even to begin to describe what happened this afternoon. Then I look up and realize Laura is watching me in her rearview mirror.

"Let's, um, talk in a little bit?"

Amber follows my eyes to her mom's and nods.

We talk about school and her soccer game. As we drive over rolling hills, past trees with leaves that are cascading in color, I feel some of my stress start to dissipate. I crack my window to let some of the crisp breeze in.

In no time, we pull up the driveway of the orchard, tires crunching over gravel. Laura and Nico tell us they're going to run some errands, and they'll be back for us in a couple hours.

When I get out of the car I'm met with the familiar and comforting smell of apples and apple cider donuts, which are baked on-site.

Amber and I walk over to the register booth, where Cleo, a senior, is working. Her aunt, uncle, and cousins own and run the orchard.

"Usual basket for you two?" she asks.

"How do you remember our usual baskets every year?" Amber asks.

Cleo laughs. "The same way I remember that you ask how I remember your usual baskets every year. Your friend is by the Honeycrisp apples."

"And how do you know where my friend is?" Amber asks, further perplexed.

Cleo cranes her neck out of the booth and points up one of the rolling hills. "She's right there."

"Oh, right. Come on," Amber says, tugging on my shoulder. "I want to know what the heck is going on!"

We walk past rows of other apples—McIntosh, Gala, Jonagolds—and finally, we arrive at the Honeycrisps. As we approach, Evie examines an apple, then tosses it into her basket. She looks at us, lost in thought. "Is it Miami?" she asks by way of greeting.

"Is what Miami?" I say.

"I thought it was New Orleans?" Amber says. She's put her basket down and is trying for a bright red apple just out of her reach.

"What are you guys talking about?" I ask.

"We still don't know where the new guy is from," Evie says.

Amber says, "However, we need to table that discussion, because something happened to Lucy today and I don't know what it is and I might explode if I don't find out immediately!"

"Tell us how you really feel," Evie says. But she stops what she's doing, a curious look on her face, waiting for me to talk.

"There was sort of a little . . . incident at the shop today," I say slowly.

Amber frowns. "What do you mean, *incident*?"

"A pie-in-the-face incident?"

Evie looks at me blankly. "Is this a euphemism? Isn't the expression an omelet on your face?"

Now I feel my face going blank, and then say, "It's egg on your face! That's the expression!"

"Okay, whatever, so the egg on your face, is that what you mean?" Evie asks.

"No, I really do mean pie in the face."

"Explain," Amber and Evie say at the same time.

"It's the funniest thing!" I try to force a laugh but nothing comes out.

My friends are still staring at me.

"So it turns out Jack Harper's parents own the Java Junction across the street. I got really mad when he told me and I sorta accidentally threw a pie in his face." The words tumble out like a waterfall.

Evie laughs so hard she snorts. "I'm sorry, but it almost sounds like you said you threw a pie in Jack Harper's face."

I laugh with her. "Because I did!" I say, still laughing.

"I'm so sorry!" Amber says loudly. "There must be something wrong with my ears. Because it really sounds like you're telling me you threw a pie at Jack Harper. And that would just be so insane!"

"Heh, yeah, your ears are actually working fine—"

Evie's mouth opens and closes a few times. "Just to be clear, we're talking about the same Jack Harper who you said is so good-looking he didn't even seem like a real human being?"

"Yes," I say in a small voice.

"And the same Jack Harper with those crazy green eyes," she goes on.

"Not like he has crazy eyes. But like they're crazy beautiful?" I trail off, remembering the way he looked at me with those eyes, the way he smiled at me, the way he offered to let me borrow his book. I feel a blush spreading across my cheeks, and then I remember the way his face looked with pie all over it, and the gravity of what I've done starts to sink in.

"LUCY! What have you done? I have at least three thousand other questions, but I'm going to start with that one. What have you done?" Amber says.

I huff, feeling suddenly impatient. "I already told you. His parents own the Java Junction across the street. You know, the one that could put my mom's shop out of business? He had the audacity to come in there, acting like he was just stopping by . . ."

Wait, why *was* he there? Did he ever say? I shake my head, forcing myself to focus.

"I'm sure he was stopping by on some kind of recon mission from his parents," I continue. "He didn't say, but that must have been it. Anyway! After he had the nerve to show up, then the nerve to tell me about his parents owning Java Junction, I sorta accidentally threw a pie at his face."

"See, you had me until the pie-throwing thing. What on earth would make you do something so, so . . ." Evie struggles for the right word.

"Oh come on, you're telling me you wouldn't do the same thing?" I feel my impatience growing. "If someone was threatening to put your parents out of business and then that person showed up and acted all nice and . . ." I pause, then sigh. "I did a stupid thing, didn't I?"

"No, no, let's not use the word *stupid*. Remember *stupid* is a stupid word!" Amber pauses. "Impulsive. Emotional. Intense," she offers.

"*Extreme*," I say, groaning.

"I wouldn't dismiss that word, either, no," Evie adds.

"Gee, thanks," I say sarcastically.

"It's the truth!" she says. "What kind of pie was it, anyway?"

"What difference does it make?" I ask, running my hands through my hair. "Pecan."

"And you threw it at him when he told you about his parents owning Java Junction." Amber is speaking slowly again.

"No! I threw it at him after he told me about his parents owning Java Junction *and* after he gave me some backhanded compliment about how our pie is so much better than some mini pie or something that Java Junction serves."

"That doesn't sound like a backhanded compliment to me," Amber says.

"Are you seriously defending him?" I sputter.

"No! Not at all! Well, maybe a little. Just . . . maybe he didn't have horrible intentions when he came in?" she says carefully.

I glare at her. "He's evil. His parents' company is evil."

"Okay, okay, let's just agree to disagree on that point. I still have at least 2,310 questions." She's choosing her words carefully again. "What happened after you threw the pie at him?"

"Ha!" I say so loudly that Amber and Evie jump. "That's the most ridiculous part. He laughed. He actually laughed!"

"Like a shocked laugh, and then he got mad?" Evie asks.

"No! Like a genuine happy ha-ha kind of laugh. He thought it was funny. Then he pretended like it was all a plan—like it was part of a school play we were practicing for."

Evie's eyebrows crinkle. "Really?"

"Really! That's weird, right?"

"Maybe a little," she admits. "I mean, throwing a pie at someone is usually used as comic relief in a movie or TV show. And think about pie-throwing competitions."

"Pie-throwing competitions?" I ask. "Is that really a thing?"

"Isn't it? I feel like I've seen people running around throwing pies at each other somewhere. Maybe it was a dream?"

"Focus, Evie," I say.

"Right, right," Evie says. "Oh! Follow-up question: Where was your mom for all this?"

"She was in the back when it happened, but she came out when she heard Jack laughing."

"So are you grounded for life?" Evie asks.

"No," I say. "That's the other weird part of it all. She seemed to think it was funny at first. And then she just sorta got serious again. Not mad, though. And then she told me to go apple picking."

"Hmm," Amber says, tapping her chin. "Well, not mad seems like a good sign."

"Yeah. But, I mean, she can't exactly ground me since she needs my help at the shop," I point out.

"Right," Evie says. "Okay, so your mom is not mad, and you are likely not grounded. Those are good things. A good foundation for this situation."

I groan. "I don't want a foundation for this situation. I don't want this situation at all."

Evie ignores me. "So if you're not grounded and your mom isn't mad, what exactly are you upset about?"

I look at her in horror. "Are you kidding me? I'm upset because Jack Harper could right this very second be posting what I did on social media, and he's going to make me come across as some sort of unhinged girl, and you know how small Briar Glen is. Remember when Jason Morris—"

"Peed the bed because he was so scared of the ghost stories!" Evie quickly realizes what she's saying. "Not that this situation is comparable to anything that happened with Jason Morris. This is totally different."

I groan again.

"Have you checked his socials?" Evie asks.

"No!" I say. "I don't know if I want to."

"Oh, don't be a weenie," Evie says.

"Weenie, really?" Amber says.

Evie ignores her and pulls out her phone. She taps around and says, "Everything is so locked down. I can't really find anything."

"So why don't you friend him so you can see if he says anything?" Amber suggests.

I look up. "Are you serious? Friend him so I can watch him say ridiculous things about me, and then watch other people say ridiculous things about me?"

"Okay, I see your point. Wait, why are you so convinced he's going to say something online, anyway?" Amber asks.

"Duh, because it's so completely ridiculous! Wouldn't you? He was probably snapping selfies while he cleaned his face up," I say, the panic rising again.

"Hold on, hold on," Amber says. "You told me he laughed, thought it was funny, but what else did he say?"

I sigh. "That's the thing. I pretty much begged him not to tell anyone what happened, and he said he wouldn't. But do you really believe him? Remember his evil parents?"

"We don't know that they're evil," Amber says.

"Will you please stop defending them!" I say sharply.

"All right," Amber says, her hands up.

"I asked him to please not say anything and he said he wouldn't. That I had his word or some other line."

"How do you know it was a line?" Evie says.

"What have I told you guys about defending him?" I snap. "Sorry. I'm a little stressed."

Amber shrugs. "Maybe he meant it? Can you let your mind go to that possible scenario for a second?"

I close my eyes. "Nope. Impossible. My life is ruined."

"We don't know that," Amber says gently. "I mean, so far he's not saying anything online—"

"That we know of!" I interject quickly.

"Right. That we know of," Evie says. "But if he had, it would have been shared by now, and it's not." She shrugs.

"So what do we do?" I ask.

"We do things the old-fashioned way. We wait. We go to

school tomorrow and see if he says anything then," Evie says.

"That's your solution?" I say, exasperated.

"I mean, short of breaking into his house and taking his phone and computer, that's kind of all we can do?" Evie says.

I sigh. She's right. I hate that she's right, but she is.

"We could also talk about what you're making for the fall festival," Amber says tentatively.

I peer at the bag of apples that I've been picking while we've been talking. She's trying to distract me. But as I start telling her about the apple upside-down cake I saw online earlier, I realize there are much worse distractions.

The Briar Glen fall festival is one of my favorite times of the year. It includes a corn maze, a mini pumpkin patch, artisans' booths, a haunted hayride, and of course, the dessert contest, which I won last year with my pecan pie. And the dessert contest includes a big cash prize. A cash prize that might end up being really helpful to Cup o' Jo's business once Java Junction opens. Not that I'm worried about or even thinking about Java Junction.

I look around. Evie's bag of apples is propped up in the grass next to a tree. Sunlight slants through tree branches, casting dancing shadows across the bag. Evie picks up the bag and I say, "Stop!"

Evie yelps and almost drops her bag. "What the heck, Lucy?" she asks, annoyed.

"Sorry," I say quickly. "Just, see how beautiful this is. I want to take a picture."

Evie waits with the bag of apples in her hands. "I kinda meant of just the apples?" I say apologetically.

"Wow, thanks," Evie says sarcastically.

"Just . . . trust me," I say hurriedly.

There is an image forming in my head. Or a feeling. Or something I can't quite put into words. A whole look. I distractedly grab the bag of apples from Evie, put it back by the tree, position it, and then snap some pictures.

I look up from my phone, with my friends watching me. "It was a cool moment," I say, struggling to find the right words. "The light was cool."

Amber pulls my phone from my hands, swipes through the pictures. "Huh. That's actually pretty cool, Lucy," she says.

Evie grabs the phone. "It was my bag of apples, could I please see?" She's quiet, swiping through the pictures, her frown fading a bit. "Okay, I see what you were doing. Or going for. I think the word is *aesthetic*," she says.

Amber says, "This would be a cool picture for Cup o' Jo's social media, you know."

I wave my hand dismissively. "We're too busy to keep our social media updated."

Amber says, "Okaaay, but, like, how long did it take you to get that picture? Maybe five minutes, right?"

"Yeah, yeah," I say quickly, impatiently. "A flawless beautiful Instagram account for Cup o' Jo. I'll add it to my to-do list."

I'm looking at my apples again. "What about mini apple tarts?"

"And we've lost her again," Evie says quietly.

"Apple cheesecake?" I snap my fingers. "Apple cider cupcakes with a caramel apple frosting?" I offer.

The rest of the afternoon at the orchard passes like this, us thinking and talking about different desserts, and I'm almost able to put Java Junction, Jack Harper, and what I did to him out of my head.

Almost.

5

Despite my fun and relaxing afternoon, I sleep terribly. I have nightmares all night of Jack going on the local news station and telling everyone that I threw a pie at his face. Then in the next dream, he's at the White House, telling the president.

I snooze my alarm too many times, and I don't make it to homeroom until right before the bell rings. I look around the room, wondering how many people Jack told about what happened, how many people know. But no one seems particularly gossipy, and no one is looking at me. I breathe a small sigh of relief. Then I remind myself it's only homeroom, and I have all day for word to get out about what happened.

But the morning feels like it takes at least a year. In all my classes, I sneak glances at everyone, see if anyone is laughing at me. But no one is. This should be a comfort, but it actually puts me more on edge because I bet Jack is waiting to say something about it online. Online, or at lunch. When I'll be in a room with half the school. When he can just push a button on his phone and half the school can find out what I did and what a weirdo I am.

By the time lunch finally rolls around at least forty years later, I'm shaking with nerves and nausea as I walk into the school cafeteria. I look everywhere, wondering if Jack is planning some kind of flash mob of embarrassment, but everyone seems to just be eating, chatting. Like a normal day.

I find my lunch table. Amber and Evie are already there.

"So how long until you think Jack tells the whole school?" Evie asks. "Maybe he's already been doing it, telling people all day. I don't have any classes with him, so I wouldn't know. Though I'd imagine the news would have started to trickle out by now. Maybe he'll do it on social media? Maybe—"

"Evie!" Amber snaps. "Not helping!"

"What?" Evie says. "I'm just thinking out loud. *And* being realistic."

Amber suddenly grabs my arm. She's been practicing martial arts since she was a kid.

"Ouch!" I say.

She releases me. "Sorry. But he's here!" she says in a stage whisper.

Evie, Amber, and I whip our heads to the cafeteria entrance, and then immediately back. "Well, that wasn't obvious or any-thing," Evie says.

"Again! Not helping!" I say.

"Just pointing out the obvious," she drones.

From where I'm sitting, I can see Jack stride into the cafeteria in that easy way he does, like he's been at Briar Glen High since his first day of freshman year. He orders something, pays for it, and then sits at an empty table.

"He's alone!" Amber says.

"I see that," I whisper back.

But not for long. Melanie flounces over to him within a min-ute, and they're talking and laughing. And for the first time in my entire life, I'm grateful for Melanie's existence. Because she's dis-tracting him from looking at his phone, from telling everyone on the internet what I did.

But as I watch them talk . . .

"Guys," I start in a panic, "what if he's telling Melanie what happened?"

I look at my friends, who are clearly thinking the same thing.

"I should have made some popcorn," Evie says dryly.

At that moment, Jack looks up. Right at me. I should look away, but I'm like a deer in headlights—in the light of Jack's eyes—so I just stare back. And then, he smiles. And waves.

I feel my own hand going up—it suddenly has a life of its own—and I'm waving back to the guy who I threw a pie at yesterday. My hand lands on the table, and I look at it, the traitor. First my mom with the pumpkin spice. Now my own body is traitorous.

Evie and Amber stare at me.

"Well, that was weird," I say finally.

And by the end of lunch, still no one, aside from my friends, seems to know about the pie incident.

The rest of the afternoon takes another forty years, until it's finally time for English class. Mrs. Ryan is asking more questions about *Great Expectations*, and I hear people giving answers, which I know, too, but I sit at my desk, staring straight ahead, afraid to even look in Jack Harper's direction.

Then we have an in-class essay to write, and that's another thirty years, and then finally, *finally*, class is over.

I'm out of my desk as the bell rings, my head down, and almost to the door. And that's when I hear it.

"Hey, Pieface, what's the big hurry?"

I glance up, and it's Jeff Griffin, a guy who can't figure out if he wants to be a jock or a bully, and who seems to change his mind every week.

But wait. "What did you say?" I ask, a block of ice now sitting in my belly.

He sneers, "I said, what's the big hurry. Pie. Face." He enunciates both syllables.

"Why are you calling me that?" I ask in a surprisingly calm voice.

"Oh, I think you know exactly why I'm calling you that," he says, looking infuriatingly pleased with himself.

I look around the classroom, for Jack, and he's still at his desk, talking to Melanie, seemingly without a care in the world.

I walk over to his desk in three quick steps. He looks up at me in surprise. "Hey, Lucy, what's up?"

"You!" is all I can muster.

He looks confused. "You okay?"

"You!" I say again.

Melanie laughs awkwardly but doesn't say anything, just looks between Jack and me.

"You said you weren't going to tell anyone! You lied! You said I had your word!"

He looks even more confused now. "I'm not sure what you're talking—"

"You know exactly what I'm talking about!" I hiss.

Then it dawns on him. "Oh. That. Lucy, I gave you my word."

"Well, your word was obviously a lie, because now Jeff Griffin is calling me Pieface."

Melanie giggles, like this is the funniest thing she's ever heard. "I'm sorry, why is Jeff calling you Pieface, Lucy?"

"It's none of your business!" I snap at her.

"So who did you tell first?" I ask Jack, my voice shaking with rage. "Please tell me it wasn't Jeff?"

Jack stands up now, and he actually looks worried. But I don't buy it. I'm not falling for it. "Lucy, I promised I wouldn't tell anyone. And I didn't. I gave you my word." And even as he says it, his eyes are still twinkling. It's good to know his eyes can still twinkle and sparkle even when he's lying.

"Well, obviously your word is a lie!" I snap back.

Then I storm out of the classroom, Jack and Melanie and Jeff and other classmates staring at me. But I don't register their faces. I don't register anything. Except that Jack Harper is a liar.

6

I send a group text on my way out of school.

Lucy

Word is officially out.

Amber

??

Lucy

I knew he was a liar.

Evie

???

Lucy

His word was a lie. Pieface is my name for the rest of my life at Briar Glen High. And probably the rest of my life.

Amber

Where are you?

And I realize I'm walking to the shop, on autopilot. But it's my day off.

Lucy

> I don't know.

I do know. Literally. I'm walking home. I'm on Pine Street, a street I've walked down a million times in my life. But mentally, emotionally, I am completely and totally lost.

My phone buzzes with another group text.

Amber

> Emergency baking session at Lucy's?

Lucy

> I can't even think about baking right now. It'll just remind me of what happened.

Amber

> You can't just never think about baking again. Thinking about the fall festival and what you're going to bake could be a good distraction? It was yesterday.

I know she's right.

Okay. Also, will give me a chance to test out some recipes that will be way better than the gross stuff Java Junction serves. 😼

That's the spirit.

Let me gather supplies. See you guys in twenty minutes?

Less than an hour later, my kitchen is full of my friends and the smell of baking apples. I started with apple cider cupcakes that are now cooling, awaiting their caramel apple frosting, and I just popped a batch of apple crumb cake muffins into the oven.

"Remind me again the difference between muffins and cupcakes?" Evie asks, reaching for a cupcake.

I lightly slap her hand away. "There are many differences. One thing that they have in common, though, is both need to be cooled to the proper temperature. Especially the cupcakes. Otherwise the frosting slides right off."

"And remind me again why fallen frosting is such a terrible thing?" Amber asks. She's got a wooden spoon out, trying to sneak a little sample of my caramel apple frosting.

I grab the spoon from her hand, tuck it into my apron pocket. "Don't you need to make sure the frosting tastes okay?" Amber asks, giving me puppy dog eyes.

"I do," I say. "But not yet."

Evie, absentmindedly thumbing through one of my mom's old cookbooks, looks up and says, "You guys should try to bring back Jell-O salads." She shows me a picture of a green Jell-O Christmas tree and wobbles it at me.

"Gross!" Amber says.

"What? Sometimes you need to think outside the box. Uh, literally, I guess, since Jell-O is in a box," Evie says.

I laugh, and then look at my hungry friends, around at my flour-covered kitchen, and I can't help but feel satisfied. There are measuring cups and bowls and whisks and bags of flour and sugar and chopped apples on every available surface. My mom had the kitchen remodeled a few years ago, and although we now have two ovens, our house is pretty old and our kitchen is pretty cozy, and we don't have a ton of counter space.

Amber is attempting to scrub some of the flour off the counter next to the sink, but she's just made a gluey, sticky mess that is spilling onto the floor. Some bakers are very tidy, cleaning up after themselves as they go. I am not one of those bakers. Neither is my mom. We prefer to completely destroy the kitchen to the point where it never seems like it'll be clean again, and then attack the dirty dishes all at once later.

Though Evie and Amber have been here almost an hour and though this was deemed an "emergency" baking session, none of us have brought up Jack Harper or my new nickname. Quite honestly, once I started mixing and pouring ingredients, the chatter in that part of my brain quieted down. My friends seemed to get that. They've seen how I am when I'm in a zone.

Now, though . . . I look up, and Amber is watching me. "It's going to be okay," she says simply.

I don't know if she means my desserts or Java Junction's opening or my new nickname, but I decide it doesn't matter. I give her a hug, and when I pull away, she's snuck the wooden spoon out of my apron pocket and is trying again to sample some of the frosting.

"You little sneak!" I squeal, but I let her try some. The cupcakes really are almost cool enough. And if the frosting needs any adjustments, now is the time. I watch her carefully. If she doesn't like something I've made, she's pretty much incapable of hiding it from me, and she knows it.

Amber turns her back to me as she samples the frosting. When she turns again, her eyes are closed in delight. "That is incredible frosting!" she says, pointing with the spoon.

"Yeah?" I ask hopefully.

"One million percent yeah," she says, as she and Evie taste more samples.

"Yep, nailed it," Evie agrees.

Just then, my mom walks in the back door, carrying groceries. She looks around the kitchen at the mess, and she smiles. "I can't wait to try these new creations!" she says, kissing the top of my head.

"This frosting . . ." Amber starts. She looks at me guiltily, a huge spoonful of frosting in her hand.

"Do you really think I didn't make extra?" I ask. "How many desserts have I baked for you?"

She laughs, and I laugh, and I've almost forgotten why we're having an emergency baking session until my mom asks, "How was school today?"

And then it's back. My new nickname. The reality that the news of what I did to Jack Harper is currently circulating around Briar Glen.

"It was fine!" I say quickly.

"Good," my mom says. "And everything was fine when you saw Jack Harper today?"

Her back is to me as she puts a container of yogurt in the fridge.

"Yep!" I say quickly.

Evie and Amber look at me in confusion. We all know I tell my mom everything. Possibly too much sometimes, according to them.

"Good," my mom says, pulling delicata squash out of another bag. "He's a good kid. I can tell. Moms know these things." She gives me another kiss on the top of the head before heading out the door, back to the shop.

My friends are staring at me, waiting for an explanation. "She's got enough on her mind with Java Junction opening soon. I don't want her worrying about some silly nickname, okay? Actually, could we just not tell her about the nickname at all?"

Amber frowns. "I'm not sure I support this decision."

"Yeah, dude, same here," Evie chimes in.

"You tell your mom everything," Amber adds. "This seems like something she'd want to know?"

I sigh. My friends are right. I tell her everything. But I also know I don't want to add anything else to my mom's list of worries. And a nickname seems like one of those things I should be able to handle on my own. It's not like I'm a little kid anymore.

I ignore the conversation and Evie's and Amber's looks. I

frost the cupcakes and hand them out to my friends, and as they chew, I slide the muffins onto their plates. They're raving about how delicious it all is, and I help myself to samples, pleased with my baked treats. But even so, everything suddenly tastes a little sour.

7

I toss and turn all night, imagining what I'm going to say to Jack the next day at school. What I'm going to say to everyone. I have to keep my cool because if I don't, it'll just make things worse for me; it'll just feed the strength of the nickname. But I wake up the next day without a plan, or any idea what to say to Jack, or to anyone. So I decide not to say anything at all, except to my friends.

I lose track of how many times I get called Pieface at school. I lose track of how many people point and laugh when they see me in class, the hallways, or the cafeteria. I ignore everyone, but still, by the time English class finally rolls around, I'm exhausted. I'm relieved that I get there before everyone else.

Everyone else that is, except Jack Harper. Who is standing at my desk.

"What do you want?" I snap.

"Well, nice to see you, too!" Jack says, his eyes sparkling.

"Are you seriously trying to joke around with me right now?" I ask, scowling at him.

Jack has a weird expression on his face that I can't figure out at first. It almost looks like his feelings are hurt or something? Well, too bad. I'm not falling for any of his lines, any of his pretend hurt feelings.

He looks over his shoulder at the door, and classmates are starting to walk in, all eyes on Jack and me.

"Look, I gave you my word. I never break my word. I promise I didn't come up with the nickname. I didn't tell anyone what happened." He looks at me desperately, talking fast. "I didn't tell anyone, but can you at least admit it's kind of funny?"

I stare at him, shocked. "Funny? Me getting made fun of is funny?"

"No! Not at all! That's not what I meant. Don't you think the situation is kinda funny? I mean, you threw a pie—"

"I know what I did!" I hiss back. "And now so does the entire school, thanks to you! And now I have this fun nickname trailing me. I'm so sorry if I'm failing to find any humor in the situation!"

He looks at me, then behind him again. More classmates are watching the scene unfold, and he says quietly, "I'll . . . find a way to fix it!"

"Fix it. Guilty conscience much?"

He runs his hands through his short dark hair, and a muscle in his arm ripples, but I tear my eyes away, look back up at him.

"Fix it because I feel bad that you feel bad because of something related to me. I don't like to make people feel bad, okay?" He's talking in a fast whisper. "Usually I like to make them happy. Especially when they are people who I might like."

And before I can say anything else, or ask him what he's talking about with this *people he might like* nonsense, he's walking back to his desk without another glance at me.

I sit down, my face burning, my head spinning. Jeff Griffin slides into his desk a few rows over and loudly says, "Did you finish the reading, Pieface?"

I glare at him, and then go back to my plan of completely ignoring everyone. Because it's much easier than trying to figure out what the heck Jack was talking about.

8

The next few days are pretty much photocopies of each other. People call me Pieface; I ignore them. I talk to my friends and avoid everyone else. So really, silly nickname aside, it's not that different of a week. Except that I *do* have the silly nickname. And there is the impending arrival of Java Junction. And then there's that confusing thing Jack said about "people who I might like." Not that I'm thinking about Jack's words. So much so that I don't even bother telling my friends what he said, and certainly not my mom, because I keep reminding myself that Jack Harper is a liar.

I also don't have much time to think about—or *not* think about—his words, though, or him, or Java Junction, or really much at all, because it's fall in Briar Glen, and I'm at the shop every day after school. Between working there and homework and school, the rest of the week passes in a blur.

I don't see anyone at the empty Java Junction storefront

throughout the week. Not Jack or his parents, no contractors. I don't notice any renovations, or a single indication that a new shop is opening anytime soon. So it must *not* be opening soon! Or maybe ever? Maybe it was a mistake? Maybe some kind of horrible joke? It doesn't matter, though, and I put Java Junction entirely out of my mind. And Jack Harper, too.

Until Saturday morning. My mom and I wake up at five again, head to the shop in our usual comfortable sleepy silence, but when we get to Main Street, a block away from Cup o' Jo, something is different. Something is wrong. Another shop is lit up. Usually on early weekend mornings, we're the only ones open. Jen's florist shop didn't open until eight.

I look at my mom in confusion, but she looks just as puzzled. We keep walking, still in silence, until we get closer to the shop. Then, my mom gasps. What used to be Jen's florist shop has been completely transformed. I don't know when or how. People, workers and customers alike, are milling around inside a coffee shop. Jack Harper, and who I guess must be his parents, are inside as well.

Java Junction is now open for business.

"Well! That sure happened fast!" my mom says. "I didn't know how soon 'soon' meant."

I'm too shocked to say anything. I just follow behind her as she unlocks Cup o' Jo's front door. I give a quick look over my shoulder at Java Junction as my mom closes the door behind her. Hard.

"Where did that wind come from?" my mom asks, a weird brightness to her voice that I've never heard before.

I still seem incapable of speech, so I just shrug.

My mom smiles, but again, it's a weird smile that I've never seen before. "Well! I was going to go over and introduce myself to Jack's parents, but clearly they're very busy!" But it almost seems like she's talking to herself.

She swings her arms, clapping her hands, and I jump.

"This shop isn't going to open itself, Lucy. Ready to get to work?"

I finally find my voice, paste on what feels like a strange smile of my own, and say, "Totally. Let's do it."

We turn on the music (Feist this morning), and my mom starts brewing coffee. Soon, Sheva and Danielle arrive, and for a few minutes the morning almost feels normal. Except that my mom keeps looking out the front window, and I keep looking at my mom looking out the window. I sneak a peek across the street at Java Junction, watching the door opening and close, watching people file in and out.

Jack is now behind one of the registers, his back to us, and I tear my eyes away again.

"Lucy, do you know what time Java Junction opens, off the top of your head?" My mom turns to me, that same strained smile on her face. "Are they just open all night?"

"I think they open at five?" For some reason I feel guilty that I know this detail, this piece of information. "Or maybe that's just at airports?"

My mom chortles. "Five a.m., that's ridiculous. How do they have the overhead for that?" But it still seems like she's talking to herself.

I see Danielle and Sheva getting the registers set up. I peek at my phone. "So speaking of opening, it's seven, Mom."

My mom is still muttering to herself and doesn't seem to hear me. "Um, Mom?" I try again.

"Hmm?" she says, looking at me, but clearly thinking of something else.

"Should we open?" I try again.

"Oh, is it time already?" she asks. "How time flies!"

"Right," I say. Everything feels so out of whack. So out of sync. I feel like I'm underwater looking up at the world around me.

My mom walks over to the door and unlocks it unceremoniously, the bell jingling quickly, almost as if it's angry. As she walks back to where I am at the counter, I realize it's the first time since I started working at the shop that she's opened without asking if I'm ready. It's such a small thing we do, such a tiny part of our routine, but it is still our routine. Our thing.

We stand behind the counter, both of us watching the door opening and closing at Java Junction.

I sneak a sideways look at my mom, but she catches me. "What?" she snaps. Then she sighs and says, "Sorry."

I'm looking at her, trying to think of what I can say or do to make things better, when our door opens.

We both turn our heads to greet our customers. Because we have customers. Because of course we do. "Good morning!" we both say at the same time.

"What can we do for you?" Sheva asks at the same time Danielle says, "What would you like?"

The customers, a group of four women, seem a bit alarmed, and one of them says, "We weren't sure if you were open yet."

I inhale sharply. "Why wouldn't we be open yet?"

My mom gives me a quick elbow jab.

"I mean, yes, of course we're open! Early bird gets the worm, and all that," I say.

"Right," one of the women says slowly.

"What can we get you on this lovely day?" my mom chimes in sweetly, now in full-on customer service mode.

They all look at the menu on the wall, and three of them order.

Danielle and Sheva make their cappuccinos and americano. I wait while the fourth one stares at the menu. Finally, she looks back at me.

"What would you like?" I ask, smiling, trying to incorporate some of my mom's sweetness into my voice.

"You know, I'm good, actually," she says.

I feel my smile start to slip a little.

"You're not getting anything, Nancy?" one of the women says to her friend.

Nancy gives me a quick glance, then shakes her head.

Her friend says, "You sure? We're going to be out and about all day."

"I'm sure!" Nancy says.

"I can get it for you, if you don't have your card?" the woman persists.

"Nope, I'm good!" Nancy says. She shoots me another nervous look.

Everyone else's drinks are ready.

"Not seeing anything that strikes your fancy?" my mom asks.

Nancy shakes her head again. "Ready, ladies?" she asks, turning to her friends.

The first woman, who offered to buy Nancy coffee, still looks confused, but she says, "Okay, let's go."

"Have a nice day!" Nancy says over her shoulder as they leave the shop.

My mom crosses her arms next to me. We both watch as Nancy opens the door to Java Junction.

I decide the milk frother needs a good scrub. And the coffee machines need to be wiped down. And we could use some more napkins out next to the milk.

I sneak glances at my mom here and there throughout the morning. She's still standing behind the counter. She's got her phone in her hand, scrolling through the news, I think. It's such an unfamiliar sight, her on her phone at work, that I realize I'm staring. As I look at her face, I realize that for the first time in my entire life, my mom seems very, very worried.

The rest of the day limps along. We do get customers. We do make sales. And we've had slow days before. Slowish days. Snowy days. Really hot days. We've just never had a slow day in the fall. Ever. Even in our weird fall blizzards, we've had customers.

I sneak glances at Java Junction here and there, and a few times it almost looks like Jack is waving at me. *Waving at me!* The nerve. His parents mill around the shop, too, but I don't let myself watch them or anything at Java Junction for too long. I can't stay still, and I bustle around the shop, wiping down surfaces I've already wiped down at least three times, organizing the refrigerator again. I sneak looks at my mom here and there, too, who in contrast to my inability to stay still seems incapable of movement. Every time I look at her, she's standing by the register, scrolling through her phone. It's such an unfamiliar sight—such a worrisome sight.

After lunchtime, three women come in together. Tourists. I ask what I can get them, and they peer at our menu, two of them murmuring to each other, and one says, "Actually, we're good. Sorry!"

"Not a problem!" my mom says, just a little too loud.

The third woman says, "I'll take a vanilla latte. Large. And"—she looks around the pastry case—"this muffin, and a cookie. Oh, make that three cookies, actually."

I pull her pastries out for her, and Danielle makes her drink. The woman's two friends have already left the shop, and she's our only customer. I ring her up, and when she swings the tablet back to me after paying, I see that she's left a one hundred percent tip.

I look at her in surprise. We've gotten big tips before, especially around the holidays, but usually from people we know. "Have a nice day!" she says, smiling. "You guys keep up the awesome work."

I'm too stunned to say anything, but my mom swoops in, saying, "You too. Thanks for stopping by!"

As the door closes behind the woman, the bell jingling, my mom looks at me. "You okay, Lucy? You're a little pale."

"Oh, she just left a very . . . generous tip," I say.

My mom's brow wrinkles. "How generous?" she asks.

"A hundred percent tip?"

My mom's face goes from shocked to happy to mad to sad all within the span of three seconds. "That was very nice of her," she finally says, nodding.

I want to ask her if it was nice why does she look so upset, but two more tourists walk in.

They wander over to our case of baked goods, muttering to each other quietly. "What's this one?" asks one of the women, pointing to the maple scone that is clearly labeled a maple scone.

As I pull out their pastries, I notice that one of the women is carrying a Java Junction cup. Danielle checks them out at the register. My mom is next to her, watching the transaction. "You know, I think I'm going to take some inventory," she says.

I watch her walk to the back of the shop, then turn back to the customer with the Java Junction cup. The woman sees what I'm looking at and blushes a bit. "Their pumpkin spice lattes are really good," she says, almost apologetically.

I'm too tired to go on my pumpkin spice latte rant and don't have the energy to offer to make her one myself, so I don't say a word. I just watch her and her friend leave the shop. Then I send the meanest possible glare my face knows how to make over to Java Junction. It actually hurts a bit.

Jack is too busy at his register to notice me or my glare, which just makes me glare even harder.

Just before closing, our door jingles open, and Jack Harper walks in. Jack Harper . . . and his parents. Danielle and Sheva have gone home already, but my mom and I are at the register, and my mom grasps my wrist for just a second before saying to them, "Well, hello! I've been wanting to come over and introduce myself all day, but we've both been so busy!"

And Jack's parents? They smile back. They actually smile! "It's so nice to meet you," Jack's mom says, walking over to our register. "I'm Erin. Jack has told me so much about you, Lucy." She's still smiling, her hand out to shake mine, and I shake her hand. I want to pull my hand away immediately, but her hand is warm, and I see where Jack gets his twinkling green eyes from, and wait, what has Jack told her about me?

I shoot him a look, but he's just beaming at me, like this is the happiest day of his life or something.

"It's, uh, nice to meet you," I say awkwardly.

My mom steps forward, shaking Erin's hand, too. My mom is awesome at customer service. She can make conversation with anyone about anything, can turn on her charm instantly when she needs to. But she actually seems genuinely happy to be meeting Erin. I'm so confused. Did she forget who this woman is?

Jack's dad steps forward now, too. "I'm Greg," he says. He's got salt-and-pepper gray hair and hipster dad glasses. He gives a quick wave to my mom and me, and then looks at his wife. And the way he looks at her, with something like admiration on his face, and Jack is still smiling, and right, they look happy because they think they're going to take Cup o' Jo down.

"Wow, you guys really picked a location!" I snap.

The happy, easy mood in the shop shifts just a little. Like the first cold wind on an otherwise sunny, warm summer day, which signifies a huge impending storm.

My mom grasps my wrist again, gives me a meaningful stare, and says to the Harper family, "This is such a great part of Main Street. Some people prefer the western part of Main Street, but we're closer to the mountain here, and obviously I'm a little biased, but I don't think you could ask for a more perfect location for a coffee shop with this view!"

I look at her in horror. Why is she being so nice to these people?

I glance at the Harper family, see that Greg is watching me. He looks uncomfortable. His discomfort makes me feel slightly better, and I smile at Jack, who is still just standing there like we're all at Disney World or something.

Erin quickly says, "I really hope you don't think we set up shop here as a way to try to compete with your business or anything. We know that Cup o' Jo is a Briar Glen institution, and we'd never want to try to take that away from you. That's the last thing we want to do. Our family has so much respect for your business. Me especially," Erin says, looking at my mom. "You opening this shop all on your own, raising your daughter all on your own; it's just so admirable!" she says.

I narrow my eyes at her. My mom is not someone who needs *her* admiration. My mom had me on her own, the way she wanted, and she opened this shop on her own, the way she wanted.

As if reading my mind, Erin says, "Whatever your situation is, of course. I'm not trying to be nosy, either! It's just inspirational. That's all I mean. Whew, I gotta stop talking!"

My mom smiles back, but some of the warmth has disappeared, and I'm reminded again of the beginnings of a summer storm. "That's all very kind of you to say, Erin. Thank you. And like I keep telling Lucy, Java Junction and Cup o' Jo are really quite different from each other. At Cup o' Jo, customers can order a drink or food totally unique to Briar Glen. And at Java Junction, customers can order a drink or food they can find anywhere, right?

Because some people find comfort in that familiarity. That predictability." She smiles a bright smile, but I see something like fear starting to form in Greg's eyes.

"We should probably get back," Greg says, touching Erin's arm.

Erin hesitates just a second and says, "Yeah, you're probably right. Anyway, it was actually Jack's idea to stop by, to say hi and introduce ourselves. I'm so sorry we didn't do it sooner!"

Jack's idea? Likely story. "Yeah, busy day for you guys, huh?" I say. But I smile, mimicking my mom's own sweet smile.

Erin looks confused. "Oh, yeah, that. I also meant we didn't know for sure when we'd even be opening. So much red tape to get through with Java Junction headquarters, some miscommunication. Anyway, we'd planned on stopping by before opening day, but we didn't know today would actually be opening day until about ten p.m. last night!"

My mom says, the warmth back in her voice, "No worries. I get it."

I spin to look at her, but she's avoiding my eyes. She does? What does she know about red tape or corporate headquarters?

Erin smiles back, looking relieved, and Greg looks slightly less scared, and Jack is still just standing there, eyes twinkling. "See you guys soon," Jack says, with such ease in his voice. An ease, I hate to admit, that breaks the awkwardness that is beginning to seep into the room. His parents leave the shop, and just before the door closes behind Jack, he says, "See you at school, Lucy!"

"Yeah, see you!" I say back.

But the door closes behind him and he crosses the street with his parents before I have a chance to remember that Jack Harper is a liar and not to be trusted.

9

The next morning, Sunday, I wake up to my mom gently shaking my shoulder, then opening my curtains, letting in the early morning fall light. "What are you doing?" I ask, my voice still raspy with sleep. Usually we just let our alarms wake us up, do our own thing until we get ready to walk to the shop.

I let my eyes adjust for a second and realize my mom is already dressed. I grab my phone. "Mom, it's only four thirty," I say, covering my face with my pillow.

"It's only thirty minutes earlier than usual," my mom says. I hear her opening my closet. "What are you going to wear today?"

"I don't know, clothes," I say, still under my pillow.

"Should I pick them out, or do you want to?"

I take the pillow off my face. "Um, Mom? I'm not in first grade?" I say. I think that was the last time she chose my outfits. "What is going on?" I ask, finally sitting up.

"I was just thinking we could push our opening time a little bit earlier. Especially on fall weekends," she says.

She doesn't need to mention Java Junction's name, so even though it physically hurts to be up so early, I yawn and say, "Oh, yeah, that makes sense."

Then I grab the flannel shirt and jeans my mom is holding out to me, shuffle to the bathroom, and try to wake up.

Despite our best efforts, we only make it to Cup o' Jo about ten minutes earlier than usual, but my mom seems happy, chipper, even, as we set up for the day, so I don't say anything about the time. Especially because today, before my mom unlocks the door, she looks at me and says, "Ready?"

"Ready," I say, and smile, feeling suddenly chipper myself, our morning tradition back in place.

And we remain chipper throughout the morning, because we're busier than the day before.

At some point during the morning rush while my mom is making a cappuccino for Liz, who she went to school with, she looks at me and smiles, and I smile back, and if I just don't look across the street, I can pretend that Java Junction and Jack Harper don't exist.

But then the next customer orders a pumpkin spice latte. I flinch for just a second, but bite my tongue and make the customer's drink. It's not the best drink I know how to make, and I know it'll by no means live up to the cult following of the pumpkin spice latte at Java Junction, but the customer smiles at me when they take it, and I smile back, despite myself. My mom looks at me, and even though we don't say a word to each other, I know she's proud of me, and I'm a little proud of myself, too.

It does quiet down a bit in the afternoon, which I tell the panicked voice in the back of my head is normal. We're usually quieter in the afternoons. Even on fall weekends before Halloween. It's raining lightly, and there is a fog settling across the mountain. That's why we're slow, I tell myself. Even though the weather doesn't seem to be affecting Java Junction.

Sheva has gone home, and Danielle is cleaning the bathroom. My mom and I are both behind the counter, keeping busy, her looking through her old, tattered account-keeping book, and me scrubbing the milk frother again, neither of us acknowledging Java Junction.

"So, not a big deal or anything," my mom says, breaking the silence, looking up from her book.

"Yeah, what is it?" I ask tentatively.

"Like I said, not a big deal, but we're not going to sponsor the fall festival this year."

"What?" I say. Clearly I haven't heard her correctly. "We've been sponsors of the festival for forever—"

"Exactly. So we're just going to give someone else a turn this year." She says it matter-of-factly.

"Does this have anything to do with money or Java—"

"Like I said, we're going to give someone else a turn," my mom says, more firmly this time.

"But—"

"Lucy, it's okay. Can we talk more about those apple cider cupcakes you made the other day?"

"Oh yeah, I almost forgot about those," I say, still slightly dazed.

"They're really good, honey. Really, really good. And so were the apple crumb cake muffins. It's been such a busy week I actually had it on my to-do list to tell you!"

I try to smile. I usually love teasing my mom about her to-do list. When we get really busy she even puts things like "wash hair" on her list sometimes. But I also know we haven't been that busy, that she had plenty of time to tell me.

I don't want to think about the white lie, so I say, "Thanks, Mom. Think we should put them on the menu? I can make some for this week?"

"Absolutely!" my mom says, and I smile a little bit, trying to stop thinking about the festival sponsorship.

"I think one could work for the fall festival dessert contest, too," she continues.

"Oh, right," I say, but with suddenly less enthusiasm.

"They're both delicious. On the one hand, the apple cider cupcakes are like nothing I've ever had before. Especially with the caramel apple frosting. And the apple crumb cake muffins just taste like, well, I know I say it about half our menu, but they taste like fall."

"Yeah," I say.

My mom looks at me. "Honey? What do you think? The festival is next weekend so if there are any tweaks you want to make, you might want to figure them out. We could put both on the menu this week and see which does better and that could be your entry?"

"Hmm, okay," I say.

My mom is studying my face. Usually I spend weeks preparing, baking countless versions of what I'm going to enter in the contest, making the littlest of tweaks here and there.

"What did you use in the caramel apple frosting?" my mom says, trying to get me to focus. "I feel like you had some kind of secret ingredient or something."

"Oh, molasses," I say. Then I blurt out, "What if I keep it simple this year? Traditional. Maybe something like pumpkin pie? My pecan pie won last year, after all." I don't even realize it's something I've been thinking about until the words are out of my mouth.

My mom looks surprised but says, "Sure, if that's what you want to do."

"I just, I want to get it right, Mom. The cash prize would really help—"

"Lucy, I just told you, please don't worry about our finances. The contest is supposed to be fun. I want it to be fun for you."

"How can I not worry?" I say, exasperated.

"Because you, my dear, whether you like it or not, make a mean pumpkin spice latte. You've put aside your dislike of the drink for the sake of the shop. That's integrity, Lucy."

I'm quiet for a second and then ask, "Do you think pumpkin spice lattes are going to save Cup o' Jo?"

"Like I just said, Cup o' Jo needs no saving," my mom replies, almost in a singsong voice. "But pumpkin spice lattes won't hurt anyone, either."

"Except for all those chemical additives in Java Junction's latte," I mutter.

"Ignoring that comment," my mom says, still in a singsong.

"Can't ignore cancer," I reply in a singsong of my own.

My mom laughs. "Some people think that cell phones cause

cancer, too, you know," she says, nudging my phone with her fingertip.

"Yeah, yeah, yeah, what doesn't," I acquiesce. "It's not that part that bothers me so much about the darn drink, by the way."

"Oh?" my mom says. "Care to enlighten your dear mother?"

"It's just the . . . fakeness of it. I mean, aside from the chemicals. Like the way people talk about it on social media. It's just coffee! With everything happening in the world, it seems like a silly thing to obsess over, is all, I guess."

"Honey, I have terrible news for you: You are standing inside a coffee shop owned by your mother. People take pictures of our drinks and post them on social media, too."

I sigh. "I know, I know. But it's just something about the cult-like following of the PSL. Like the peer pressure behind it or something."

"The nonuniqueness?" my mom offers.

"Yes, exactly!" I say. "If everyone likes the same darn drink and posts about it on social media, aren't we just a bunch of robots?" But this makes me think of Jack Harper again. And thinking of Jack Harper and pumpkin spice lattes makes me think of throwing the pie at him, and my nickname, and I need to redirect my thoughts, and fast, because I'm finding myself getting cranky again.

"Lucy, have I ever told you that you have an old soul?" my mom says, interrupting my thoughts.

"At least three times this month."

My mom laughs. "Good."

"You're the one who raised me, so . . . sorry not sorry?"

My mom laughs again.

"Speaking of old souls or whatever, I really think I'm going to go with pumpkin pie for the contest." Just saying the words out loud fills me with a surge of excitement. Who needs fancy new ingredients to some fancy new recipe, when the simplest answer is right in front of me in the shape and form of a pumpkin pie.

"If that's what you want," my mom says, looking into my eyes. "And I mean it! I don't want you doing what you think is best for the shop, what you think is most likely to win the cash prize. I want you to make what you want to make, for *you*, okay?"

"Okay, okay," I say impatiently, avoiding her eyes.

"Lucy." My mom holds my face, forcing me to look into her eyes.

"Got it, got it," I say, hoping she won't notice that behind my back, I'm crossing my fingers.

10

"Hey, Pieface," someone says to me while I'm on my way to homeroom the next morning. I don't even know who it is because I'm digging through my backpack, making sure I wiped off all the flour from my homework. After my mom and I closed up Cup o' Jo yesterday, we had a mini baking session. I tried to talk more about the sponsorship, but she was having none of it. Instead, we tweaked the ingredients of the apple crumb cake muffins and apple cider cupcakes until they were exactly to our liking. I also made a pumpkin pie, for good measure. And we may have made a slight mess, and some of it may have made its way onto some of my homework.

"Hey," I say back without thinking or looking up.

The person stops. "She answered to it! She answered to it!" the voice says to no one in particular.

I look up, annoyed. Of course. "Seriously, Jeff?" I snap. "Do you really have nothing else going on in your life?"

"Not as much as you do, Pieface," he says.

I sigh, rolling my eyes. "And what, exactly, is so exciting about my life?"

Jeff seems to lose a little bit of his steam. "Well, I don't have a nickname for throwing a pie at someone!"

"You do not," I say, my attention back on my homework.

"Because you threw a pie at Jack Harper. Because you're . . ." he trails off, even more steam lost.

"Because I'm weird, Jeff?"

This conversation isn't going the way he wanted at all.

"Yeah! Only weirdos throw pies at people!" He's talking louder now, looks around the hall, and Jayden Lochman saunters by. "Right, Jayden?"

Jayden stops, and he's practically beaming with delight. "Well, well, if it isn't our resident Pieface," he says.

"The weirdo Pieface," Jeff chimes in, nudging Jayden with his elbow.

"Keep up the good work, boys," I say, finally mostly satisfied with the state of my notes. I pat them both on the shoulders before I go to homeroom. Pumpkin spice lattes and silly nicknames. Two annoyingly predictable parts of my life now. But somehow neither is bothering me that much today.

And I'm not even that annoyed about the sponsorship thing

anymore, either, because I totally nailed my pumpkin pie recipe last night. After last year's win, I can almost taste this week's victory—picture the winning contest money in Cup o' Jo's bank account.

My good mood carries me through the rest of the morning, until lunchtime. I sit at my table with Evie and Amber, and I think I'm whistling. Except I don't really know how to, so maybe I'm not. But I feel like I should be whistling.

Evie eyes me suspiciously. "What the heck are you so excited about?" She pauses, then whispers, "Pieface."

Amber jabs her, and I say, "No, no, it's fine! It's just a silly nickname! As predictable as the day is long that some kids will tease someone about something so ridiculous, with such a silly nickname."

Amber puts her hand to my forehead. "You feeling okay? Remember that whole emergency baking session we had because you were so upset about the nickname? Because you were so upset about what happened with Jack?"

"Ah, that is where you are wrong, dear bestie!" I say. "I was upset about the nickname, and I am no longer."

"You're talking weird," Evie says.

"Guys, it's just a silly nickname!" I say.

"And you're just okay with Jack Harper, too?" Evie shoots a

look over her shoulder, and I follow her gaze. He's just walked into the lunchroom.

I inhale sharply, then look back at my friends. "Never said that!" I realize I'm gritting my teeth. "He's still a lying liar who lies, but I have other things to think about."

"Okaaay," Amber says.

"Holy cow, what is going on already?" Evie asks. "I feel like I'm in the Upside Down or something."

"Nothing is going on. That's what is so wonderful," I say.

Evie says to Amber, "Can you make her be normal, or at least get her to tell us what is going on?"

"Guys! The fall festival is this weekend! Did we all forget about that? Like the best weekend in Briar Glen," I say impatiently.

Evie shrugs. "It's cool, but aren't we getting a little old—"

"The corn maze, the pumpkin patch, the bonfire, c'mon, aren't you guys a little excited?" I persist.

"I guess," Evie says, but she still looks confused.

"And the dessert contest!" I say.

"You finally figured out your recipe!" Amber says, recognition dawning on her face.

"So, what did you decide?" Evie asks eagerly. "Those new muffins, or the new cupcakes? They're both so good. The judges will love them."

"Neither," I say, feeling the wind deflate from my sails just the tiniest bit.

Evie and Amber share a look of uncertainty.

"I'm keeping it simple this year. Classic this year. Because, ahem, who won last year's contest?"

Evie says, "Oh my god, just spit it out already! What are you making?"

I take a deep breath, spin my phone around, and show them a picture of the pumpkin pie I made last night. I put the pie on our pumpkin dish, and as I look at the picture now, I realize it's actually a pretty good picture. I mean, as good as a picture of a pie can be.

My friends silently peer at my phone.

Evie finally says, "That looks like pumpkin pie?"

"Because it is!" I say.

"Okay," Evie says. "But I thought you were going to try something different this year."

Amber says, "Did you make it with, like, a sweet potato crust or something?"

I wrinkle my nose. "Blasphemy!"

Evie says, "So it's just a regular plain old pumpkin pie."

"I think *classic* is the word I think you're looking for, dear friend," I quickly retort.

"Your pumpkin pie is amazing!" Amber says. "And you won last year's contest! I'm sure you'll at least be a finalist, if not the winner!"

"Finalist," I scoff. "Finalists don't earn cash prizes. Just gift cards to the tourist shops."

"Since when are you so interested in a cash prize?" Amber asks.

"I'm going out on a limb here and saying it's because of Java Junction?" Evie says.

"Java who?" I smile sweetly at the table, then take a huge bite of my sandwich.

Amber looks at me. "Does your mom know why you're entering a pumpkin pie in the contest?"

"Does she know I'm entering a classic, timeless pie in a contest I want to win, you mean?" I ask innocently.

Amber groans. "Lucy, those desserts you made for us last week were really good. Are you sure—"

"Blasphemy!" I repeat.

Evie and Amber share another look, which I ignore. Or try to ignore. Because somewhere in the back of my brain a little seed of doubt is starting to sprout. Just the tiniest of seeds. But it's still there. Like my nickname, like Jack Harper, I decide to ignore it.

"What time do you guys want to meet on Friday?" I ask, trying to keep my chipper mood intact.

"It's only Monday?" Evie says.

"Never too early to start planning!" I say.

Never too early to figure out how to avoid Jack Harper this weekend, either.

II

It turns out it never *is* too early to start planning. We always close Cup o' Jo on the Saturday of the Briar Glen festival and set up a tent at the park grounds, and every year I forget how many details we have to figure out and plan for.

And despite Java Junction's sudden appearance in Briar Glen, and despite Jack Harper seeming to be everywhere all the time at school and across the street from me when I'm at Cup o' Jo, it's impossible not to be excited about the fall festival. It really is one of my favorite weekends in Briar Glen. I think it's a lot of people's favorite weekend in Briar Glen.

Customers are buzzing about it all week, and by Friday afternoon, everyone at school is talking about the festival, when they'll go, with whom. Because even though there may be just the tiniest bit of hokeyness to the festival, and maybe we are getting a little old for some of the events, even the stereotypical popular kids still like a good haunted hayride. I mean, who doesn't?

When I get to English class on Friday afternoon, Jack is standing by my desk. I've managed to avoid talking to him all week, so I frown when I see him.

"What are you doing here?" I ask.

"A pleasure to see you, too, Lucy," he says, laughing.

"Don't you mean Pieface?" I shoot back.

And as if on cue, Jeff and Jayden say, "Oh, look, Jack and Pieface are talking. Watch out, Harper, I hear her aim is impeccable."

Jack ignores them but still doesn't say anything to me.

"Yes?" I say slowly.

"Oh, I was just, um, wondering if you'll be at the fall festival this weekend?" he asks.

"Why, so she can throw some more pies at you?" says Jayden, laughing.

Jack keeps ignoring them, and so do I.

"Yeah, the whole town kinda goes?" I say, confused. It seems like something he would have gotten a memo about by now.

"Right, right, I was just wondering because—"

But then Mrs. Ryan walks into the room, telling everyone she knows we're excited about the weekend, but we need to sit down and get started on our in-class essays.

I'm so focused on what I'm writing, and then the bell is

ringing, and it's the weekend of the Briar Glen fall festival, officially! I pack up my books and head to my locker, but it's not until I'm closing the door that I realize I never figured out what Jack wanted to tell me.

I work a blur of a shift at the coffee shop, and then it's time for the start of the festival! Amber and Evie show up at Cup o' Jo a few minutes after five thirty. Danielle and Sheva are already gone, but my mom is still cleaning up, still making a few last-minute preparations for the next day, so I'm hesitant to leave her, but she just about pushes me out of the shop, and my friends just about drag me out.

"Have fun!" my mom practically commands.

"Okay," I say. "I won't be out too late, and I—"

My mom turns to Amber and Evie. "Can you make sure she has fun?"

They laugh and nod, and I give my mom a quick hug, before she gives me another gentle push out into the cool fall night.

All up and down Main Street, our old-fashioned lantern lights have been lit. A few shops extend their hours for the festival, and locals and tourists alike mill about. The shops keep their doors open, music playing. A lot of kids are in Halloween costumes, and some shopkeepers are handing out candy.

It's a clear night, and the stars are out, and it's impossible to deny there is magic in the air as we head to the park. A group of kids dressed as PJ Masks characters run past us, their Halloween buckets rustling with candy wrappers. Their parents, who I recognize from the coffee shop, trail behind. They used to come in a lot when their kids were first born, babies strapped to their chests, always looking slightly shell-shocked and really, really tired. One of the parents, Mary, has twins, and I was amazed at how effortless she made it seem, and she never failed to thank my mom and me for having a changing table in the bathroom. Lauren, another parent, keeps saying "Say thank you" every time her daughter, Tavey, gets candy.

My friends and I are laughing about something. I don't even know if we know what we're laughing about, but it doesn't matter. The closer we get to the park, the more we can smell the bonfire, and the more the air seems to fill with excitement.

And then, we're officially at the Briar Glen fall festival. I grab Amber's hand, and I squeal—a sound I think I only make here. She squeezes my hand back, and I see the excitement I feel reflected in her eyes.

The festival is set at one of our town parks. Although I've been going to this park and its playground my entire life, every fall festival weekend the space seems to transform into someplace different—somewhere fantastical. The first night of the festival features live music from a couple local bands, a few food tents, and a bonfire. We can see the bonfire, smell it, and one of the bands has just started to play on the small raised stage where the dessert contest is tomorrow, but I'm not thinking about it, of course.

It's the same scene every year, and the band is the same local cover band that's been playing for at least the last five festivals. The drummer is Evie's neighbor, and the guitarist teaches band at the middle school. But still, maybe my friends and I do walk a little more quickly this year, and maybe we're laughing again and I'm still not sure why. And maybe that's okay.

We're still laughing when we get to the bottom of the hill. And that's when I stop. Stop moving. Stop laughing. Stop breathing. Because hanging from the streetlamps, flapping in the wind, are the sponsorship flags with words on them. WELCOME TO THE 25TH BRIAR GLEN FALL FESTIVAL. PROUDLY SPONSORED BY JAVA JUNCTION.

Evie is wearing only a hoodie and keeps walking toward the bonfire, but I grab Amber's arm and point at the flags. "Did you know about this?"

"Oh, yeah, I think I might have heard something about them sponsoring the event. I'm not sure," Amber says quickly, her hand on my back, guiding me away from the flags and toward the bonfire.

She's not meeting my eye.

"You have got to be kidding me!" I shout. A few people walking by turn and give me curious looks.

"She's just really cold!" Amber says, once again guiding me away from the flags.

"Tell me the truth: Did you know about this?" I ask accusingly.

"Know about what?" Amber says, sounding suddenly tired.

"That Java Junction was going to weasel its way into the fall festival?"

"Lucy, I don't think there is really any weaseling going on. I think—"

"What did I tell you about defending Java Junction?" I snap.

Amber puts her hands up. "I'm not defending them. Hasn't Cup o' Jo been a sponsor, like, a million times?"

"Yes!" I say quickly, leaving out the part where my mom seemed to be hinting that we couldn't afford to sponsor the fall festival this year. "But we never weaseled our way in."

Amber says, "I'm pretty sure sponsorship involves no weaseling. Or ferreting or mousing or anything else rodent related."

I smile, but I give one more look at the flags. "Can you at least admit it's a bit much that Java Junction is sponsoring this year's festival? Like, really, of all the years? Can you admit that at least?" I'm aware that I sound desperate, but I can't help it.

Amber sighs heavily. "Fine. I'll admit it. It's weird that they're sponsors this year. Now can we please get to the bonfire already? I'm freezing!"

"Fine, fine," I say, giving one last look at the sponsorship flags before Amber and I head to the bonfire.

The fire itself is pretty small—there are too many nearby dry leaves and trees for anything big—but still, every year, something about the bonfire always seems so otherworldly. Maybe it's the smell of the smoke from the firepit, the way it'll linger on my coat for days after; maybe it's seeing the shadows of the flames dance across everyone's faces, how different everyone looks in the fire-light. Even though I know every single local at the fire, and have known them my entire life, something about the bonfire makes them seem mysterious. It reminds me how many sides there are to all of us.

After Amber and I get to the fire, we quickly find Evie. I see some of the excitement I feel reflected in my friends' eyes, and as we talk about bonfires from years past, Halloweens from when we were kids, Jack Harper and Java Junction and its sponsorship fades from my mind.

Evie says, "So you're still set on pumpkin pie for tomorrow?"

"Yep!" I say. "I'm making the pie tonight, so it'll be super fresh for the judges."

Maybe it's just a shadow from the flames, but I swear that Evie looks disappointed for a second.

I say quickly, "Pumpkin pie is a classic. And like I said, the judges usually like classics, like my pie last year, and Annie Elliott's apple pie a few years ago, and . . ." I try to remember all the contest winners over the years but am suddenly drawing a blank . . . and suddenly having serious second thoughts about my dessert choice.

"Hey! Her pumpkin pie is awesome!" Amber says quickly. "Remember?"

"Oh, no doubt, it's delicious!" Evie says.

"Thanks," I say, but I can't seem to get warm, even being so close to the fire.

Now I can't remember what my friends and I found so funny on our way to the festival, what we were laughing about.

"You guys want to check out the music?" Amber asks.

Evie groans. "Do we have to? It's just Elise and Mr. Stange and their friends, and we've been listening to them for years. Plus it's so nice and toasty by the fire."

My eyes are tearing up, and I wipe them quickly. Amber is watching me. "The smoke is making my eyes water."

We both know I'm lying, but we both ignore the lie.

"Cover band or not, I wouldn't mind checking them out," Amber says.

"Well, then, what are we waiting for!" I grab Amber's and Evie's hands as we head toward the stage.

The band has just started playing "Brown Eyed Girl," and Evie and I are laughing again, because my mom loves to tell a story about how some guy she went on a few dates with changed his ringtone to "Brown Eyed Girl" because my mom has brown eyes (just like me).

We laugh and dance and spin and sing, and some of the night's magic returns. Even when I hear someone shout, "Wow, Pieface has some moves!"

I don't know who the voice belongs to, and it doesn't matter because I'm with my friends and we're dancing, and it's a beautiful night, and that's all that matters. That's what I want to remember from this night.

After a while, when the band slips into some long instrumental riff, Evie, Amber, and I wander back to the bonfire. As we get closer, I realize I see someone else at the fire. Jack Harper. He's talking to Crystal and Angela, who are both juniors.

"How about some hot cocoa instead?" I offer.

My friends follow my eyes and say, "Sounds good!"

But it's too late. "Lucy, Amber, Evie!" Jack says, waving his hand, calling us over.

The three of us look at one another, and Crystal and Angela look at us, so I whisper, "Let's just get this over with."

"Hey, guys," Jack says as we approach.

"Sorry, I only answer to Pieface," I say to Jack.

Jack starts to smile, but then he looks at me, Amber, and Evie and quickly stops.

"We were just talking about *To Kill a Mockingbird*. I already read it freshman year, but they were saying it's a junior-year book at Briar Glen High," Jack says, filling the silence.

"So what's next for your family?" I ask Jack, keeping my eyes on the flames from the bonfire.

"What do you mean?" he asks, sounding confused.

"Well, let's see, first you guys move in across the street from Cup o' Jo, then you're sponsors of the Briar Glen fall festival. Is your mom going to run for mayor next?"

I tear my eyes away from the fire, look at Jack. Then I remember earlier, in English class, when he was by my desk. "Is that what you were going to tell me today?"

"I don't think the sponsorship is a huge deal. My parents just—"

"Not a huge deal?" I say. "Are you kidding me?"

I'm aware of Crystal and Angela watching the conversation, of people turning to look at us, and across the fire I can see Jayden Lochman's smirking face.

"You know what, I don't want to hear any more." I turn to Amber and Evie. "We were on our way to get some hot chocolate, anyway, weren't we?"

"Right, we were," Amber says awkwardly.

"Yeah, see you later," Evie says.

I don't say anything else to Jack Harper, and I stride away from the fire with my friends.

"You okay?" Amber asks softly when we get in line at Bob's hot chocolate tent.

"Just peachy!" I say, forcing a bright smile.

Amber says to Evie, "I was trying to explain to Lucy that the Java Junction sponsorship isn't a huge deal."

"And I was trying to explain to Amber that it *is* a huge deal, and that everywhere I look, I see Jack Harper, or Java Junction!" I snap back.

"Lucy, I don't want to argue."

"I don't, either. That's why we agreed that'll you stop defending Jack Harper and Java Junction."

"I wasn't defending either of them, I was just—"

"Hey, girls, it's almost our turn!" Evie says. "What kind of hot chocolate do you want?"

"Hot chocolate, the same kind Bob has been serving for years," I say.

Evie sighs. "I mean, do you guys want whipped cream? Marshmallows?"

She knows I always order hot chocolate with one marshmallow and a ton of whipped cream, and Amber, the weirdo, just likes her hot chocolate without any of the toppings, but Amber makes a big production of trying to decide.

We place our order, pay, and Trish, Bob's wife, hands over our hot chocolates in paper cups.

With the words JAVA JUNCTION printed on the side.

I feel Amber and Evie looking at me out of the corner of my eye. But I take the cup. I will not let Jack Harper or Java Junction take away any more of the magic of this weekend. I will not let him win.

The hot cocoa does taste more bitter than I remember, though.

We take our hot cocoa back to the stage, where a band from the next town over is playing. Amber dances in place, lightly bumps her hip into mine, trying to get me to move, but it's hard to dance while drinking hot chocolate, and the microphone keeps squealing with feedback.

I look over at Evie, realize she's shivering in her hoodie.

"Do you guys want to go back to the fire?" I shout, just as

the squealing stops, the music stops, and I'm suddenly speaking very loud.

"What was that, Pieface?" I hear a voice from somewhere behind us shout.

I take a deep breath, keep my eyes on Evie's face, and she says between chattering teeth, "Okay!"

"Great!" I say, and with my friends by my side, we leave the stage area.

I shout over my shoulder, though, to the anonymous voice, "That name doesn't even make any sense!"

We walk away before the person, whoever they are, has a chance to reply.

But the fire is dying down, too, and our hot chocolates get cold fast. Evie is still shivering, and as much as I hate to admit it, our first night of the fall festival is over.

On the walk home, Amber tries to re-create some of the enthusiasm and energy we had on the way over, but it doesn't work, and Evie is so cold that she ends up calling her dad, and he gives us all rides home.

I blame Jack Harper for this bitterly cold end to the evening.

12

My mom comes in my room early the next morning, cracking the curtains. "Seriously, again?" I ask, yawning. "Two weekends in a row? Is this a new tradition or something?"

"Well, it can be a fall festival tradition if you want," she says cheerily.

At her mention of the fall festival, everything from the night before comes crashing back to me. My mom frowns. "You feeling okay?" she asks, putting a tentative hand to my forehead. "Usually you're dragging *me* out of bed on festival weekends."

"Yeah, I'm fine," I say in an obviously not-fine voice.

My mom waits for me to go on.

I sigh heavily. "Did you know that Java Junction is sponsoring this year's festival?"

"Maybe? Someone might have told me. It's not really that big of a deal. Like I said, it's our turn to share the sponsorship! Is that what has you—"

"Don't say I'm cranky," I warn.

My mom laughs. "Deal. Is *tired* okay to say?"

"That's fair game," I concede. She gets up to leave, and I say, "But, Mom, even Bob's hot chocolate tent's cups had the Java Junction logo on them. Isn't that, like, overkill?"

"Honey, I think you're thinking too much. And *I'm* thinking you need to hurry up if we want to get the Cup o' Jo tent set up at the festival on time!"

She's right. I will not let Java Junction or their annoying sponsorship interfere with any more of my life or with any more of the fall festival weekend. I will not let them take anything else away from me. I will not let Jack Harper take anything else away from me.

I hop out of bed, and soon my mom and I are on our way to the fall festival to set up our tent, just like we have since I was a little kid. We're in my mom's Subaru, the trunk loaded up with our batch brewer, coffee, paper cups, napkins, and an assortment of pastries, including the apple crumb cake muffins and the apple cider cupcakes. And in my lap, I'm protectively cradling the pumpkin pie I made last night before I went to bed. It's in a travel pie carrier, yet I still wrap my arms around it.

It's a cold morning, and the car has just started to heat up when we get to the parking lot. We're the first ones here. My mom and I sit in silence in the front seat for a moment, watching the sun, which is just starting to come up and is casting a beautiful glow through the amber and burnt-orange leaves and across the field.

But we both keep watching the dashboard clock, and finally, we both look at each other, knowing we really have to get things set up.

I ignore the Java Junction sponsorship flags on our walk in, and my mom doesn't say anything about them, either. The setup is relatively quick, and by the time we're done, other vendors have arrived, the morning has started to warm up a bit, and as I look around, some of the excitement I felt the night before has started to return.

We're next to a tent selling fresh apple cider donuts from Lynn's, our local grocery store, and the smell is intoxicating. My mom buys us one each, and my donut is still warm as I bite into it.

"Now this makes it feel like the fall festival," my mom says, sighing.

My mouth is too full of donut, so I just nod.

As I'm savoring my last bite, we have our first customer. Emily Hutz, whose daughter, Becca, is in my math class. She orders a coffee, and just like that, our day takes off. Our drinks aren't too complicated since we don't have all our supplies and gadgets with us, but still, by ten we've had a steady stream of customers, a mix of regulars from our shop and tourists visiting Briar Glen.

The dessert contest table is next to the stage, and between customers, I watch people drop off their entries. It seems like more people than in years past. I have until noon to drop off my pie, so I don't know what I'm waiting for. Or why I suddenly feel nervous.

"Go drop off your pie already!" my mom says.

"Okay, okay!"

I carefully pick up my pie and walk slowly over to the dessert table. When I get there, wow, there are even more entries than I realized. I don't ever remember seeing so many before: vegan surprise chocolate cake, snickerdoodles, apple coffee cake, and more. Then I look at my pumpkin pie. I think again about Amber's and Evie's faces when I told them about my entry, and I start to panic— just a little, though, because the judges usually favor classic, simple desserts, and surely this year can't be any different . . . right?

I fill out the entry form, give my pie a little protective pat, and whisper "good luck" to it before I head back to the Cup o' Jo tent.

When I get there, Amber and Laura and Nico are chatting with my mom, and such a regular, familiar sight makes some of my nerves dissipate. It's just a normal morning at the fall festival; nothing depends on my pie winning any contest.

"There she is!" Amber says when she sees me.

"You guys just get here?" I ask. *Just a normal morning*, I keep telling myself.

Amber stretches and yawns dramatically. "Yep. I slept in late this morning, so we haven't been here too long yet. Just did one loop around."

"Brat," I say, poking her and laughing.

"I know," she says. "I won't mention the pancakes we had."

"Fine, then I won't mention the Lynn's apple cider donut I had," I reply, still laughing.

"Double brat," she says.

"Lucy, Amber, you guys go enjoy yourselves! Yes, you too, Lucy," my mom says, giving me a pointed look.

"Are you sure—"

"Yes!" my mom, Amber, and Amber's moms all say back at once.

"All right, all right," I say. I take off my Cup o' Jo apron. "What about packing—"

"It's why we're here," says Nico.

"Now shoo!" says Laura.

"And have fun!" says my mom.

I grab my bag and my jacket, and Amber and I wander off.

Amber yawns again, and I poke her again. "We're meeting Evie by the corn maze. Good morning?" she asks.

I think for a second. "Yeah, it was, actually. We were busy!"

"And did you drop off your pie?" she asks.

"Oh, was I supposed to drop it off?" I ask her.

She sticks out her tongue at me, and we find Evie waiting for us at the maze.

"There you guys are!" Evie says. "Thought maybe you went in without me."

"I think you would have noticed," I say.

"Fair point," Evie says, and we all laugh.

It's hard to call the corn maze much of a maze, really—it's stacks of hay and some random stalks of corn—but it's never stopped us from going in and having fun before. Evie heads into the maze ahead of us, and Amber and I lag behind.

But something is different now. As I look at Evie in front of me, so tall among the little kids, most I've known since they were babies, something—some fireball of emotion—has landed right in my chest. I'm thinking about the PJ Masks costumes last night, all my Halloween costumes from when I was a kid.

Amber is talking, but when I look at her, she stops. "You okay?" she asks.

"Yeah," I say uncertainly. "Just . . . do you ever feel yourself nostalgic for a moment you're living in?"

Amber frowns, looks around at the maze. "Not sure I'm following."

"We've been coming to this festival our entire lives. Remember when the maze used to seem so huge and scary? When the bales of hay towered over us? When we were their size?" I point to the little kids in front of us.

Amber laughs. "I don't, because remember I was too scared to go in until I was, like, seven."

I remember how proud she was when she went in the maze for the first time.

"Those moments, these moments, they can't last forever, can they?" I ask slowly. "They'll be over someday. Someday—someday soon—we're all going to be at college, and what if we don't live in Briar Glen and—"

Amber gently turns me to face her. "And we'll always have these moments, Lucy. These moments, these memories, they're here." She taps her chest, close to her heart. "And here." She taps her head.

I nod but don't say anything.

"Are you sure you're okay?" she asks me.

I look again at Evie ahead of us, then at the laughing little kids, remembering when they were babies, and also remembering when I was their size. But finally I decide to take my friend's advice and tuck the memories away into my head, and my heart. "Yeah, I am," I say. And I mean it. I think.

After three trips through the maze, we're all a little thirsty, so we go to the food tent area and get some fresh apple cider from Lynn's, then cruise through the pumpkin patch for some shameless selfies. The pumpkins are all brought in from local farms, not actually grown in Briar Glen, and okay, it's a little hokey, but it's also part of the nostalgia that is suddenly hanging around me like a necklace.

We've all been checking our phones, eyes on the time without needing to acknowledge why, and finally, it's almost two—almost time for the dessert contest winner to be announced.

"Ready whenever you are, babe," Evie says, looking at me. "Should we go find some seats?"

"Sure, yeah," I say, distracted.

Evie looks at me, a confused expression on her face. "Wait, are you nervous?"

I see Amber looking at me curiously, too. Being nervous about anything baking related doesn't really compute with them, or with me, really.

"Yes. No," I say. "Yeah, okay, maybe a little. The, uh, cash prize is more enticing than usual this year?"

Amber frowns. "Does your mom know yet why you're so invested in the contest this year?"

"Maybe?" I lie. Half lie. "But we should find a place to sit. It's filling up quickly!"

Amber is still frowning, but we head to the dessert contest area, and once again I can't believe how many desserts are on the table.

I hear my friends saying the same thing as we find some seats near the stage. The judges are just starting to arrive at their table, which is on the side of the stage. The first judge, Ms. Brooks, my elementary school principal, has been a judge for the contest for as long as I can remember. The second judge is our town librarian, Mr. Shea. They sit down, chatting, looking at all the desserts in front of them.

The third judge is someone different every year. One year it was our town's fire chief; another year it was the owner of the diner. Sometimes it's a surprise judge; sometimes it's not. This year, I realize I don't actually know who the third judge is, so I guess it *is* a surprise.

And what a surprise it is. Jack Harper quickly slides into the empty judge's chair.

My mouth drops open, and I turn to Amber and Evie, trying, and failing to speak. "What is *he* doing up there?"

Amber looks just as shocked as I feel.

"This is a joke, right? Or a bad dream?" I ask Amber. "Isn't it, like, a conflict of interest?" I protest. "Can Java Junction be a sponsor and also a judge in the pie contest? Isn't that, like, a monopoly?"

Amber doesn't have time to answer any of my questions, though, because the microphone crackles to life as the Briar Glen mayor begins talking.

And it finally dawns on me: This is what Jack was trying to tell me in English class yesterday and at the bonfire last night. Not about the sponsorship, but about him being a judge for the dessert contest.

But I can't hear what the mayor is saying. The words aren't sinking in. I catch something about how this year has the most entries the town has ever seen, with some desserts the judges have never heard of before, what a difficult decision it was, and could the following three finalists come to the stage?

I don't even hear my name, don't even register that the mayor has said it, until I feel Amber jabbing me with her elbow. "Get up there!" she says, smiling.

I nod and float to the stage. I recognize the two other contestants: One is Autumn Joyner, a woman who owns the local Pilates studio and is one of my mom's friends, and the other is Liam Wilkerson, a kid a few years older than me, who graduated from Briar Glen High last year or the year before. We look at one another and smile. Ms. Joyner gives me a little wave, and I wave back. Liam nods at both of us, and then the mayor is talking again.

I look at the judges' table, still not fully processing that Jack Harper is one of the judges. Even as Mayor Porter introduces Jack, even as Mayor Porter says he's the son of the new Java Junction owners, which I swear some people boo at. Jack waves to the crowd, then looks at me, waving and smiling, like this is the happiest day of his life.

I smile back at him, a reflex, for a split second, maybe less. Or at least I think I do. Because seeing Jack here now, I'm reminded again of my lovely new nickname, and of how completely untrustworthy he is. Reminded of why I want—no, *need*—so desperately to win the contest this year for Cup o' Jo.

An icky feeling is starting somewhere in my stomach as I listen to Mayor Porter praise the complexity of the finalists' desserts, the work and creativity that clearly went into each recipe.

"We received so many great entries this year. Many things I'd never even heard of, things I didn't even know existed until today!" He rubs his stomach. "I may have sampled a few myself. It's been an educational day for sure. But alas, there can only be one winner. Please know that the judges said this was the most challenging competition they've judged to date, and there may have been some . . . disagreements among the judges along the way."

Jack looks at me, and something about his expression makes me feel worse. Is he looking at me with something like . . . pity?

I try to ignore him, to focus on what Mayor Porter is saying, but suddenly I don't want to hear anything he's saying at all.

"And the winner of the contest is . . ."

I'm having a hard time hearing him over the thump of my blood pressure in my ears.

"The vegan surprise chocolate cake, made by Autumn Joyner, owner of Shining Brightly Pilates studio!"

My heart drops to my stomach.

I clap, but it's like I'm watching someone else clap. And then I'm walking off the stage, but it's like I'm watching someone else walk away, too.

Someone is saying, "Lucy, where are you going?" But I don't know who Lucy is or where she's going.

The same someone is grabbing my arm, and I think it's Amber, but I say, "I'm fine! I just need some space."

And then I'm walking, but I can't say with any certainty if I can feel the ground beneath my feet.

I keep moving, at least I think I do, until I get to the artisans' tents. A candle maker waves at me. She's Shasta's mom, another sophomore. But my eyes can't focus. I don't know if I wave back. I do know that I keep walking until I'm behind all the tents, in a weird sort of hallway, where the two rows of artisan and food tents back up to each other. I have a sudden memory of playing in this same space when I was a kid, pretending I was in a magical hallway that could take me anywhere and everywhere in the world. Right now, I'd like to go back to a Briar Glen that exists without Java Junction, or Jack Harper.

And then, as if I willed his presence, Jack is standing a few feet away from me. He gives a tentative wave, but my arms feel like they're made of metal, way too heavy to pick up, so they just stay by my side.

We just stare at each other. I think of his face, the way he smiled at me with pity when I was standing with the other finalists. And then I flash back to when he came to Cup o' Jo the first time, when he tried my pie. Was he lying then, too? Did he just pretend to like the pie? Of course he pretended. He pretended to like the pie, and then today, in today's contest, he made sure someone else would win. That I would lose. That has to be what happened.

Something stings my eyes, and I realize I'm crying. My steel arms are incapable of wiping away my tears.

Jack walks slowly toward me, concern splashed across his face. "Hey, are you okay?" he asks, his voice soft.

"This is your fault!"

"What?" Jack looks confused.

"Don't play innocent!" I say, my voice getting louder. One of the jewelry vendors pops open her tent and gives me a curious look.

I grab his arm, pulling him behind one of the food tents, where the noise from the hissing griddle will block out our conversation.

"Anyone ever tell you you're really strong?" Jack says, rubbing the spot on his arm that I grabbed.

"Yes. My mom tells me all the time," I quickly reply.

Jack laughs, but I just glare at him. "Cool, so my strength is funny to you?"

Jack looks alarmed. "No, not at all. I just—"

I interrupt, "I don't want to talk about my strength. I want to know why you sabotaged the dessert contest."

"What? What are you talking about?" He still looks confused.

"Look, I know it was stupid to throw a pie in your face. You didn't have to lie, though, tell me it was no big deal, and then make up the stupid nickname and lie about making up the stupid nickname—"

"I told you, I didn't start the nickname! I agree, it's totally stupid! It makes no sense. I'd like to think if I made up a nickname for you it'd be slightly more creative than Pieface."

I feel my rage dissipate for just a second. I shake my head. "No, that's not what this is about. What this is about is you sabotaging the contest so I would lose."

"Sabotage? Seriously?"

"Yes, *sabotage*," I say, liking the dramatic effect of the word.

"Lucy, I have no clue what you're talking about," he says. "Why would I sabotage the contest?"

"I don't know. You tell me!" I sputter. "Are you jealous of my mom's coffee shop? Threatened by us? I didn't tell you guys to open Java Junction across the street. It's not my fault that we have a loyal customer base, that tourists and locals love our shop."

The words falter in my throat as I think about some of the slower days we've had at the shop lately.

Jack is shaking his head. "Lucy. Listen. I love the pie you made for the contest. I was trying to convince the other judges yours was the best. But they had their minds set on the chocolate cake. I think because it was vegan. I don't know. I loved yours, though. Really."

I look at him, the earnestness in his eyes. "Whatever," I say, but I suddenly feel deflated.

"If anything, I felt a little jealous," he says.

"Jealous?" I say dubiously. "Of what?"

"Your baking! I could never make anything like that."

I feel my cheeks flush a bit. "Thank you," I say quickly. "It's not that hard, though."

He laughs. "Not that hard, yeah. You *just* make pie good enough for a dessert contest, *and* make pie and muffins and cupcakes that your mom sells at her coffee shop. No big deal."

I will not accept his compliments. I cross my arms across my chest. "Well, when you bake pumpkin pie a million times it's not hard anymore," I finally say.

"Are you bragging?" Jack asks, with a twinkle in his eye.

I feel my cheeks heat up. "What? No! Being proud and confident is not the same as bragging. Are you some kind of guy who can't accept strong, confident girls? Seriously?"

"No! Not at all!" Jack looks truly horrified. "I love your strength and confidence. I mean, I love when girls are strong and confident."

"Oh, because it's such a surprise when we are?" I snap back.

"No!" Jack says. "Lucy! That's not what I mean at all. Of course girls and women are strong. Dudes could never handle giving birth." He waves his arms wildly. "Listen, this is getting all twisted up. I was just trying to say I loved the pie. Really. The bragging comment was lame. It was my lame attempt to try to make you feel better. I'm pretty lame."

"Yeah, you are!" I say, louder than I mean to.

Jack looks hurt, and I feel a teeny tiny bit bad.

"Can we go back to the part where you tell me how awesome my pie was and how you didn't set up the contest so I would lose?" I say.

"Gladly," Jack says, the twinkle returning to his eye. "Sabotage," he mutters.

I smile a bit.

I watch Jack, wonder how he gets his eyes to do that, and the smile starts to fade from his face just a bit. He clears his throat. "I'm sorry you didn't win the contest. You should have. I voted the heck out of it. And really, I wish I could make pie like that."

I give a quick nod. "Thank you. You're possibly maybe slightly redeeming yourself."

And then we just look at each other. "What do you, um, bake?" I ask. Suddenly the silence feels like too much. Too twinkly.

He bites his lip. "I don't really bake much." I can't say for sure, but it almost looks like his cheeks are flushing. Is he embarrassed?

"I mean, I know I bake an abnormal amount, like almost every day, sometimes multiple times a day, but when you do get the chance to bake, what do you make?"

Okay, he's definitely blushing now. "I don't really bake at all?" he says uncertainly.

"At all, at all?" I ask, confused.

"At all, at all," he says, but now he won't meet my eyes. "I don't actually know how to. How to bake."

"Seriously? Your parents own a coffee shop and you don't know how to bake?"

"The baking is all taken care of off-site. We just reheat the baked goods when they come in," he says, softly, like he's ashamed.

And the twinkling moment is gone. It all crashes back down to earth again. Java Junction across the street from Cup o' Jo. Our suffering business. I look down at my hands, realize they're shaking. "You know, you should have entered some of Java Junction's stupid desserts in the contest. They're gross, but who cares? Who cares that your company already makes a bazillion dollars. Why not give the prize money to you guys as well. Let's just let the rich keep getting richer." I almost spit the last part I'm so angry.

I look at Jack, ready for him to fight back, ready to challenge whatever he says next, but he's got some expression on his face I can't quite figure out. "It's the prize money," he says quietly. "That's why you wanted to win the contest so badly."

"Wanted? Needed!" I'm shouting, but I don't care, about anything. I glare at him, my eyes blazing, then turn to go.

"Wait!" Jack says quickly.

"What?" I snap, spinning back on one heel.

"Maybe I can help you?" he says.

"Help me? You've got to be kidding me! I am not some charity case. My mom's coffee shop is not some charity case!"

"No, listen, Lucy, that's not what I mean." He's talking fast. "I mean, maybe I could help you guys with your website. With social media stuff. I may not know how to bake, but I've done some social media stuff for Java Junction."

I scoff. "What business has time to constantly update social media?"

"Um, a lot of them, Lucy? It's the 2020s. You're a teenager. I know you're on social media."

"You do?" I ask.

"I mean, I'm assuming you are! Who isn't?"

I wonder for just the briefest of seconds if this means he's looked me up. Not that it matters. Not that I care.

I narrow my eyes at him. "Why do you care about Cup o' Jo's social media?"

He sighs. "I'm just saying, you guys could increase your online presence. It might . . . help things," he says delicately.

"You know what would help things? If your stupid coffee chain hadn't moved in right across the street from my mom's shop!" I feel lighter, getting the words off me. They'd been sitting on me so heavily for so long.

Jack's voice is soft again. "Lucy, like my parents said the other day, they didn't open the Java Junction across the street from you guys in some evil attempt to drive you guys out of business. They spent a really long time researching different areas where a Java Junction could go. Months. The entire time we lived in Atlanta that's all we were doing. They were doing virtual tours of cities, taking weekend trips to random places all over the country."

"Your poor parents. How they must have suffered," I say mock sympathetically.

He sighs again. "I'm not trying to get your sympathy! I'm just trying to say your pie is really good. I wish I could bake like that. I wish I could take lessons or something. Okay?"

I feel a slight sense of pride, but then remember who I'm talking to. "Why, so you could put my pie on Java Junction's menu and take away more of our sales?" But somehow, in some twisted way, I think I almost mean it as a joke.

He gives me a small smile. "Yes, that's exactly it. Remember that part where we talked about how all of Java Junction's gross desserts are made off-site and reheated?"

I smile now. "Perhaps."

He shrugs. "It'd be cool to learn how to bake, is all. My

parents love to bake in their spare time. I guess I haven't always understood the appeal of it? One of my cousins is a pastry chef. Another is in culinary school! I feel like the black sheep of the family when it comes to baking, or something."

"That's a new one," I say. "Feeling like a black sheep due to one's baking ability." I tap my chin thoughtfully, lost in my own memories of baking with my mom during my childhood, and all throughout my life, how good it felt, how good it still feels.

He sighs again, looks at me with that earnestness. And it dawns on me: I realize he's not going away from Briar Glen. I can't will away his presence. I can't will away Java Junction. Maybe the best thing to do is stop fighting, stop pushing, and just . . . accept him and Java Junction? Maybe I just need to stop letting him get to me?

"I'll give you one baking lesson," I say, surprising both of us.

"Really? Are you serious?" He looks more than happy, almost excited?

"Really," I say. "It goes against my best judgment, but I guess you caught me in a charitable moment. Plus, I look forward to endlessly teasing you about how little you know about baking."

"Nothing, remember? Not a thing."

I give a little laugh. "Maybe this could be fun?"

"You look a little evil right now," Jack says.

"Good," I say, then throw back my head in soft maniacal laughter. The idea of knowing more than Jack suddenly, absolutely thrills me.

When I look at Jack again, he looks amused. And hopeful? "So, can we agree to a deal? You teach me how to bake, and I help you with your social media? And not because I think you guys need it. It's not an act of charity or something," he says, registering the flash of doubt that I can feel.

"Fine, something like that," I say. Against my judgment—and anger and frustration at Jack Harper and Java Junction—I shake his hand, agreeing to his deal.

"I should, uh, get back," he says. "I'm sure my parents are looking for me."

"Me too," I say. While we've been talking I've been vaguely aware of my phone buzzing with texts. When I pull it out of my pocket, it's filled with texts from my friends and my mom, asking if I'm okay.

But still Jack and I stand there just a second longer, looking at each other.

"See you later?" he finally says. "At the festival or at school?"

"Yes, right," I say. I watch him walk away, wondering if I've just made a huge mistake.

I wander over to the food tents, my friends' location according to their string of texts. They're sitting on what used to be a barrel at one of the food tents, backs to me, eating warm oversized pretzels dusted in cinnamon sugar from Briar's Bakes, our local bakery. Another Briar Glen fall festival food tradition, and I smile at all the memories, all the pretzels we've eaten throughout the years.

Amber must feel my eyes on her because she whips around and sees me. "There you are!" she says. "We were worried."

"Not worried enough to stop yourselves from getting pretzels, though, I see," I say teasingly.

"Stress eating," Evie says through a mouthful of pretzel.

"Are you okay?" Amber asks, her eyes serious.

"I'm okay!" I say.

Amber looks at me, clearly not believing me, and I say, "I am! I swear."

Evie says, "Okay, so we've established that you're okay, apparently, but *where* were you?"

"Talking to Jack Harper."

Amber drops her pretzel.

I scoop it up. "Ten-second rule?"

Evie smacks it out of my hand. "Goose-poop rule!"

"And, uh, yeah, I find it a load of goose poop that you're okay," Amber says, looking at me suspiciously. "And I thought you said Jack Harper was essentially full of goose poop himself? Remember that whole thing where I couldn't defend him?"

"Enough with the goose poop!" Evie says, her mouth full of pretzel.

"Oh, sorry," Amber says.

She looks at me, waiting for me to explain myself. "I realized I wanted to win the contest for the wrong reasons," I start. "I sorta lied to my mom about it, too, which karmically is maybe why I lost? And also, it proves that she was right, that I shouldn't be so afraid to try new recipes, new things. I totally should have entered those apple cider cupcakes or apple crumb cake muffins in the contest."

"You had all these epiphanies in twenty minutes?" Evie looks at me with a raised eyebrow.

"While talking to Jack Harper," Amber chimes in, looking at me skeptically. "The same Jack Harper who you said was a lying liar."

"Yeah?" I say, shrugging. "Oh, I also agreed to give him baking lessons. Well, one baking lesson."

Evie drops her pretzel this time, but no one reaches for it.

No one says anything for a few seconds until Evie says, "Okay, I'll bite. Not the pretzel on the ground. What the heck is going on?"

"With what?" I ask.

"With everything!" Amber and Evie say at the same time.

I sigh. "Okay, I know it all sounds bananas, but hear me out. Like I said, I had the wrong reasons for entering that pie in the contest. I was too focused on the cash prize."

"Right, we've already established that," Amber says impatiently.

"Yeah, I'm waiting for the part where you explain why you're conversing with the enemy?" Evie says. "The person you were just so convinced was trying to bring down all of humanity?"

I shoot her a look.

"Okay, or at least Briar Glen," she says sheepishly.

"Maybe the only way to beat the enemy is to accept him?" I say.

"Okay, Yoda," Evie says.

"No, I just mean, like, he's not going away from Briar Glen. I'm tired of letting him get to me. Of letting him win, or whatever. All of the energy I'm expending on him. Of giving him the power. I'm taking back the power!" I say, shaking my fist.

"By giving him baking lessons?" Evie says, looking sadly at her pretzel on the ground.

"One baking lesson," I correct.

Evie says, "Wake me up when we're out of the Upside Down, okay?"

"Oh, he also offered to help with Cup o' Jo's socials," I say in a rush.

Evie says, "Honey, I love you, but I can't keep up with you."

Amber says, "It sounds like he wants to help? Like he's taking the same approach as you? A solidarity, of sorts?"

"Yes, exactly!" I say. "I knew at least one of you would get it."

"Gee, thanks," Evie says.

"If you can't beat 'em, join 'em? Or something?" I say, looking at Amber.

"Right!" Amber says. But I catch the uncertainty in her voice. And once again, I start to wonder if I've made a huge mistake.

13

Sunday morning, I wake to the sound of rain hitting my bedroom window. I stretch in bed and think about falling asleep again. My mom insisted I take the day off from Cup o' Jo, bringing in Rachel, a college kid who helps out at the shop here and there. A sleepy Sunday does sound especially luxurious, especially a rainy sleepy one.

But it's the last day of the festival, and my friends and I have never, ever missed the last day—even the years it's snowed or rained—so I stretch one more time, and then start a group text asking when everyone wants to head over to the park.

My phone remains oddly quiet. It's after ten, so Amber and Evie should be awake. But I look again outside at the rain, tell myself maybe they *are* still asleep.

I take a long, hot shower—another luxury I don't often have on weekends—and I expect to find a string of texts from my friends, making our plan for the day. Still, nothing. It's almost eleven now, and the festival only goes until three on the last day. Suddenly, I feel irritated.

Lucy

Okay, I'm ready when you guys are?

A few minutes later, my phone finally buzzes.

Evie

I'm wiped. Fall festivaled out.

Amber

Same.

Lucy

Guys, it's the last day!

Evie

I'll go!

Lucy

No, it's okay. Don't want you to turn into a popsicle again!

Amber

I can go for a little bit. Been wanting to try out my new Wellies.

Lucy

Be at your place in ten?

She sends back a thumbs-up emoji, and my irritation fades, and I feel okay.

That sense of okayness doesn't last long. When I get outside and open my umbrella, I realize it's not just raining. It's freezing raining. Frozen wet ice pellets hit my umbrella. But I'm wearing my winter boots, so my feet are nice and warm, which is all that matters, I tell myself as I turn onto Amber's street.

Then an ice pellet somehow makes its way into my sleeve, and I shake my wrist, trying to get it out. Wet sleeves are another nemesis of mine, and as I ring the door to Amber's house I feel some of my earlier irritation sneaking back.

Amber opens the door, and I must look as irritated as I feel because she says, "What's up with you?" Then she peeks around me, and says, "Is that freezing rain?"

"Yes," I say, shaking my sleeve again. My now cold, wet sleeve.

"You know we could just skip the festival—"

"No!" I say. "It's the last day. We never miss the last day! We go every year!"

Now my irritation is starting to turn into a weird sort of sad panic, and Amber says, "Why don't you come in for a second?"

"No!" I say again. I know I sound like a brat, and I think I even stamp my foot. "We have to go, otherwise we're going to miss the end of the festival!"

"And what happens if we miss the end of the festival?" Amber asks gently.

"It's one of the last years we'll go as students, like actual residents of Briar Glen, and . . . and . . ."

"And you want to remember the end of this year's festival as us being cold and freezing and miserable?"

I know she's right, but I say, "We could just go for a little bit?"

"And do what?"

"I don't know!" I sigh. "I don't know," I repeat, quieter this time, and I realize I'm close to tears.

"If you really want to go, one of my moms can drive us?" she offers. But I can hear how half-hearted the offer is.

"No, no, it's okay," I concede. "It's disgusting out here. You're right."

"It *is* disgusting out! So why are you still out there? Come in!" Amber says, opening her storm door. "We can watch a movie or something!"

But it just feels wrong. Everything feels wrong. "No, I think I'm just going to head home."

Amber peers around me again. "Okay, but let us at least give you a ride?"

"No, that's silly," I say. She lives only three blocks away from me. "I'll see you at school tomorrow, okay?"

"Are you sure?" Amber says uncertainly.

I nod quickly, then turn to go, before she can see the tears that have inexplicably started falling down my face.

I walk home, the freezing rain mixing with my tears.

14

The next day at school, Jack is waiting for me at my locker with a book under his arm. "Um, hi?" I say, turning my head, trying to see what book he's holding.

"How was the rest of your weekend?" he asks, like we have these kinds of conversations all the time.

"Fine?" I say.

The confusion I'm feeling must show on my face because he says, "Oh, I realized you don't have my phone number."

"Your phone number," I echo, still confused.

"Ohhh, good morning, Pieface!" Jayden trills in an annoying falsetto as he walks by.

I take a deep breath. The stupid nickname is another thing I can't do anything about. What's done is done. The nickname is here to stay, just like Jack and Java Junction. At least this is what I tell myself as I roll my eyes.

"You know that whole 'baking lesson slash I give my stellar

social media advice' thing we talked about yesterday? Pretty sure it wasn't a dream." Now I see a new expression on Jack's face I haven't seen before. It almost looks like he's . . . unsure of himself. Nervous?

"It was Saturday," I say. "We talked about it on Saturday." I don't know why I feel the need to point out his mistake.

The nervous, unsure look is gone from Jack's face as quickly as it appeared. "Yes, Saturday. Anyway, I figured it'd be easier to set up details over text than at school."

"Pieface!" Jeff shouts as he walks by.

"Gee, why would you ever think such a thing?" I say, rolling my eyes again.

I hand him my phone so he can add my number to his contacts, and he shifts the book to his other arm, so I can see the title. *The Joy of Cooking.* He adds his contact info to my phone and hands it back to me, again shifting the book in his arms. He sees me looking at the book and says, "I wanted to learn a little bit about baking before our lesson."

"You're studying before our baking lesson?" I ask. Something about the way he's holding the book makes him look so innocent and, I hate to admit it, cute.

"I suppose you could call it that. I want to be a little prepared, I guess?"

"That's really . . ." I search for the right word.

"Sweet?" he offers.

I laugh. "Yeah. For the sake of the pun, let's call it that."

"Well, see you later?" he says.

"Later, yeah," I say, in a bit of a daze as he walks away. I guess I'm still having some trouble accepting Jack as a non-enemy.

On my way to homeroom, I see his very first text to me.

Jack

Pieface.

I put my phone away, hating that I'm smiling.

At lunchtime, the first thing Amber says to me is, "I'm so sorry about yesterday." My mind draws a blank until she slowly says, "The last day of the festival?"

"Oh, right, that," I reply, avoiding her eyes.

The freezing rain and my tears had let up by the time I got home from Amber's house yesterday, and I don't feel like dwelling on it anymore, so I say, "Totally the right call! It was disgusting outside. Gave me some time to bake, too." I pop open a food storage container. "Pumpkin cranberry orange muffins!"

Amber eagerly picks one up and immediately starts eating it, but Evie just looks at hers.

"I know, you don't like raisins or cranberries or any sort of dried fruit in your baked goods," I say. "But just give it a try?"

Evie grumbles but picks up a muffin when she sees how much Amber is enjoying hers. She takes a little nibble, picks out a few cranberry pieces, then takes another nibble. Amber and I are both watching her.

"Fine! It's not terrible!" Evie begrudgingly admits.

I smile triumphantly. I'm so busy basking in my pride that I don't even see Jack approach our table. I just glance up, and there he is.

"Oh!" I say, startled.

"Did you make those?" he asks, pointing at my container of muffins.

"No, she bought them at the gas station on Main Street," Evie says sarcastically.

Amber shoots her a dirty look, but Jack just laughs. "Okay, okay, fairly stupid question with a fairly obvious answer."

Then we all just sit in an awkward silence. Well, only partially awkward because Jack is still just standing there, smiling his easy smile.

"Did you, uh, need something?" I finally ask.

"Sorry," he says. "I guess I just wanted to see the newest Lucy concoction. Wondering if maybe it's something you can teach me to make!"

I frown. "Well, we agreed on one baking lesson. Pumpkin pie, remember?"

"Maybe we can change the terms of the agreement?" Jack asks. But before I have time to answer him, he says, "See you later!" and walks away.

"I thought we said pumpkin pie?" I say weakly, but only my friends hear me.

They look at me, and Evie starts laughing, spitting muffin crumbs everywhere, and then Amber starts laughing, spitting crumbs, too.

"Guys, this is not funny!" I say. But it's hard to keep a straight face for long as I watch my friends spitting muffin crumbs, like they've turned into some sort of weird geysers, and soon I'm laughing just as hard as them.

For some reason I catch Jack's eyes, where he's sitting a few tables over, not with Melanie anymore but with some guys from the soccer team, and he's laughing, too.

I have to admit, this new not-hating-Jack-Harper thing has made my life a lot easier. Maybe even a little more fun.

I'm not dreading English class today, which is good, because it used to be one of my favorite classes. Well, before we started *Great Expectations*. Which, mercifully, we are almost done with.

I walk into the English classroom, and I even smile and wave at Jack. He looks momentarily surprised but smiles and waves back.

"Hi, Pieface," Jayden says, but it sounds quieter than usual.

Turns out not being mad at Jack makes it much easier to focus on what Mrs. Ryan is talking about, and I raise my hand to answer one of her questions. By the time the class is over, I feel lighter. Like myself again.

My good mood carries over to my shift at Cup o' Jo, and I make three pumpkin spice lattes without comment. Between customers, when I'm tidying up the pastry case, my phone buzzes.

Jack

So?

Lucy

What?

Jack

What? What?

Lucy

I think most texts usually start with a hi?

Jack

Oh right. Hi Pieface.

Lucy

Seriously?

Jack

Okay yeah, that was pretty corny.

Lucy

You said it, not me.

Jack

So!

Lucy

Oh, an exclamation point this time.

Jack

So! As I was saying, before I was so rudely interrupted.

Lucy

Yes.

Jack

Hi, Lucy. This is Jack. I wanted to see when your schedule might allow for you to give me one of the baking lessons we previously agreed on.

Lucy

Better.

Jack

So?

Lucy

I see your point. Wednesday?

Jack

Works for me.

Lucy

Cool.

Jack

So?

Lucy

This again?

Jack

So should I go to your place? Or would you rather come to mine?

Lucy

I believe the apprentice usually goes to the master?

Jack

So?

Lucy

So how about 5:00 Wednesday?

Jack

So perfect.

I text him my address, wondering once again what on earth I've just agreed to.

I look up, and my mom is watching me from the registers, an eyebrow raised.

"What?" I say quickly. "I'm sorry I was on my phone. I know you don't like customers to see us on our phones—"

"No, it's not that," she says. "I was just wondering who you were texting, because you have a huge smile on your face."

"I do not!" I say defensively. "It was a . . . business transaction."

My mom looks at me, waiting for me to elaborate.

Sigh. "I offered to help Jack Harper learn how to bake my pumpkin pie, and in exchange he's going to help with our social media stuff."

"I think you're supposed to ask before you hang out with someone I don't know? It doesn't happen much in Briar Glen. Wait, am I doing this parenting thing right?"

"You do kind of know him," I say. "Remember when you said he seemed like a good kid?"

"Yeah, that's right," she says. "But wait, I thought you didn't like him?"

"I don't!" I say. "I mean, I don't know. He's okay."

She looks confused but says, "All right, I guess this is a Mom-approved activity. Where are you giving this lesson?"

"In the abandoned house down by the river. It's probably full of loose boards with nails sticking out of them. Tetanus waiting to happen."

My mom is not amused.

"At our house," I say. "Wednesday after my shift here."

My mom shrugs. "Sure. Yeah. It's okay. I think?" She's quiet for a minute, considering something. "Why is he helping you with social media stuff?"

"Oh, he just noticed that our accounts could maybe use a little dusting off," I explain. "Increase in web traffic usually means an increase in foot traffic."

"Lucy, if I have to tell you one more time that I don't want you thinking about our sales—"

"Got it, got it."

My mom is still looking at me. I make the motion of zipping my lips shut.

"Throw away the key while you're at it, okay?" my mom says, a little smile on her face.

I nod wordlessly, and toss an imaginary key over my shoulder.

15

Before I know it, it's Wednesday, the day of my baking lesson with Jack.

At the end of English class, Jack says, "See you later?" and somehow, it feels normal. Weird new normal.

At 5:02, my doorbell rings, and I see Jack standing on my porch. I take a deep breath and let him into my house.

"Um, welcome," I say, gesturing around the small entryway.

Pancakes, the nosy creature, strolls in, stretching and yawning. She plops down in front of Jack and looks up at him.

"Well, hello," Jack says, immediately bending down to pet Pancakes. He scratches her behind the ears, and she rubs against his hand approvingly

"You like cats?"

"Why do you seem so surprised?" he asks, chuckling.

Maybe I'm not surprised he likes cats. Maybe I'm just surprised to see him liking my cat, seeing him interact with my cat, in my house. I think the weirdness of the situation is starting to catch up with me.

Jack is now sitting on the floor, Pancakes trying to crawl into his lap, and if he feels even an ounce of weirdness about anything, he's not letting it show.

"The kitchen is over here," I say. "You can pick up Pancakes and bring her with if you want. She's one of those cats who actually loves being held."

"Pancakes?" Jack looks confused.

"Oh, the cat," I say. "Sorry, I didn't formally introduce you. Pancakes, meet Jack; Jack, meet Pancakes."

He laughs. "Pancakes might just be the best cat name I've ever heard."

"I'm sure you say that to all the cats you meet," I say teasingly.

Jack follows me, Pancakes in his arms. "Wow," he says when we walk into the kitchen.

"Wow what?" I ask.

"Wow, your kitchen!" he says. He gently puts Pancakes into the window seat in order to inspect the appliances more closely.

I try to see the kitchen from his eyes—the double ovens, all the baking and cooking gadgets. I have to admit, it *is* a pretty cool kitchen. Though I'm more than a little biased.

As I watch him look around, it strikes me again how weird it is that he's in my house. But then I realize I'm psyching myself out, and that I'm psyching myself out about psyching myself out, so I start gathering baking supplies.

"Ready to get to work?" I ask over my shoulder as I pull down a big mixing bowl.

"Sure!" he says.

"You want me to show you how to make that pumpkin pie?"

"That pumpkin pie," he says, laughing. "You mean that amazing pumpkin pie that you made from scratch that should have totally won the contest!"

I can't help it, I laugh. "Jack, you know the contest is over. I didn't win. You don't have to keep—"

"Will you please just accept the compliment?"

I laugh again. "Fine. Compliment accepted. Thank you. So, here we go," I say, walking over to the sink to scrub my hands.

Jack follows my lead, lathering and scrubbing his hands, then drying them on a dish towel.

"We'll start with the piecrust," I say. "I made it last night and let it sit in the fridge overnight."

He looks at me blankly. "You made the piecrust? Like, from scratch?"

I laugh. "You really weren't kidding about not knowing anything about baking. We don't do store-bought crusts in this house."

He waves his hands around the kitchen. "Haven't we already established that's why I'm here?"

"Okay, okay," I say. "Let's get started."

He nods and, for some reason, grabs a wooden spoon.

"What are you . . . " I begin. "You know what, never mind."

I take a bottle of cream out of the fridge and a measuring cup out of the drawer and put them on the counter next to the mixing bowl. "Can you measure out one cup of heavy cream?"

He salutes me.

I preheat the oven, gather some more ingredients, and turn to watch Jack. His measuring cup is nowhere close to being at the one-cup mark, and he's about to dump it into the mixing bowl.

"What are you doing?" I ask.

He looks confused. "Measuring the ingredients?"

"Are you sure 'measuring' is the right word to use here?"

He frowns. "What do you mean? You said one cup of heavy cream, so I have one measuring cup, and it says one, and I filled it with cream."

I sigh impatiently. "Yeah, but you have to fill the whole one cup, like to the one-cup line. Otherwise, you don't have enough."

He looks at the cup in his hand. "Isn't this close enough?"

"Close enough?" I sputter. "There is no close enough in baking! Baking is a science! Every single part of it. A recipe can totally change, even by the way you stir the ingredients, the temperature of the ingredients, and certainly by how much of the ingredients you use."

"All right," he says. "I got it." He puts the measuring cup back on the counter, pours in more cream, but now it's way past one cup. He looks at me, so proud of himself.

"Did you hear anything I just said about exact measurements?" I snap.

"What? You've got to be kidding me. That's like a smidge above the line," he says defensively.

"Sorry," I say. "But have you ever seen the word *smidge* in a cookbook?"

"Well, I've never really looked at a cookbook before this week," he says.

I sigh again, then grab the cup from his hand. I slowly pour out the extra cream, and when the cup is filled exactly to the one line, I look at him slowly, not wanting to disturb the perfect measurement. "One cup exactly," I say quietly.

"Are you seriously whispering?" he asks.

I look away from my cup of cream just long enough to glare at him.

"Does the volume of someone's voice also affect how a recipe turns out?" he says.

I keep glaring at him.

"Should I sing to the cream?" He bends over, puts his face next to the cream, and in a horribly off-key voice starts to sing "Jingle Bells."

He looks at me as he sings, and when he gets to the end of the song, he lets the last note drag out, and at his big finish he flings his arms out, knocking the measuring cup out of my hand, spilling cream everywhere.

We look at the measuring cup on the floor, then at the cream around the kitchen. Somehow there is even cream on the ceiling.

"Oops," Jack says in a quiet voice. And, for the very first time since I've known him, I think he might be really embarrassed. His face is flushed as he says, "I'm sorry."

"It's fine," I say. "I'm a messy baker usually. Though this is like next-level mess. Nice work!" I say, patting him on the shoulder.

"I think you're kidding?" he says.

I laugh. "It's fine. I'll clean it up. And now you know how to measure exactly one cup of cream, right?"

"Right, okay," he says.

I clean up as much of the cream as I can, and when I turn around, Jack is kneeling, eye level with the measuring cup, slowly pouring in the cream. I feel a little proud of him.

He catches me looking at him, then looks quickly back at the cream and starts humming "Jingle Bells."

I can't help but laugh.

I have Jack measure out a few more ingredients, which he does, without any humming or singing. I show him how to mix the ingredients, how to bake the crust, how to pour the pie ingredients into the piecrust, and eventually, the pie is finally ready for the oven.

After the oven door is closed, Jack looks around the messy kitchen. "You know, this is exactly the kind of thing you should be putting on social media!" he says.

"Putting what on social media?" I say impatiently.

"All of this," he says gesturing around him.

"Again, can you be a smidge more specific?" I ask him.

"Smidge," he says. "I thought it couldn't be used as a unit of measurement in baking?"

"No, but it can be used as a measure of annoyance!" I say.

His eyes are twinkling. Seriously, how does he do that? It's like those people who can move their ears or do that weird bendy thing with their tongue. It must be a genetic thing or something.

"Lucy, I'm serious, though. This whole scene, this whole process, people on social media would eat it up."

"Eat it up? Could you try a little harder with the puns?"

"Lucy, for real. Stick some pictures up of your baking."

"Ah yes, because the crowd will go wild for a measured cup of cream," I say. I pause. "Though in your case, maybe picture by picture directions are what you need!"

He ignores that last sentence and says, "Okay, enough with the cream. But something else! Some other component of baking." He taps his chin, thinking. "What about how you come up with the recipes?"

I look at him blankly.

"Think about what inspires you to create your recipes. Where you get inspiration from. And just, I dunno, put some pictures up."

I cross my arms. "Got it. I'll take pictures of my brain and put them on the internet. Are we done with this conversation now?"

"It just seems like a perfect opportunity to show your talent. The talent behind the owners of Cup o' Jo."

Something is happening to my face. Am I blushing? But then it occurs to me. "Wait, what's in it for you? Like, you shouldn't be giving me business tips. Aren't our businesses competitors?" I ask. Something else suddenly occurs to me. "You aren't doing this because you feel bad for me, are you? Because I told you we do not need your charity—"

He looks hurt. "Lucy, I'm doing it because I care about you. Your business could do really well, and there is an opportunity right here, and you should take advantage of it. And we agreed that if you gave me a baking lesson, I'd give you social media advice. I just, I want you to be happy," he says.

"What makes you think I'm not happy?" I say defensively.

"This is coming out all wrong," he says, sighing. "Just, try something for me, okay? Get a couple pictures of this." He grins, gesturing around at the mess we've created while making the pumpkin pie.

I sigh. "Fine!"

I look around the kitchen, the way my mom's cookbook is open to a picture of the pumpkin pie we just made, the jars of spices behind it. It all reminds me of the picture I took of the apples at the orchard.

Against every fiber of my being, I take Jack's advice, and I think about all the times I've made the pie. My first memories of making it with my mom when I was little, when I climbed up the stepstool to reach the counter. All the times I made the pie for the shop, for my friends. I take a few pictures, move a few things around on the counter, take some more pictures. I thumb through the pictures, and okay, as much as I hate to admit it, maybe he's not totally wrong.

I hand my phone to Jack wordlessly.

I busy myself putting spices away, my back to him, when Jack says in a singsong voice, "I knew it. And you knew it, too."

I whip back around. "I'm not saying you're right. But I'm saying I see your point. But! You weren't the first person to think of posting some pictures to Cup o' Jo's social media account, okay?" I show him my pictures from my trip to the apple orchard.

"Yes!" he says. "Post those pictures already. They're good. They show . . . what is that word?"

"Delightful autumnalness?" I ask, smirking.

He smirks back. "No, some other word."

"I think the word is *aesthetic*?" I say sweetly. "I'll think about it, okay?"

"Has anyone ever told you you're annoyingly stubborn?"

"Just you," I say. I take a step toward him, jab him in the chest. I mean it as a joke, but the sudden physical contact, being so close to him . . . the room feels really hot. And it's not from the oven.

He looks at me, then down at my finger on his chest. The oven beeps. We both jump, and say, "The pie!" at the same time.

I grab the oven mitts off the counter. For some reason, my hands are shaking as I open the door. I try to stop the shaking as I pull the pie out, then carefully slide it onto the wire cooling rack. Even though I know from experience that the pie is done, I insert a toothpick to make sure. I pull out a perfectly clean toothpick, toss it in the trash, then turn the oven off. All without looking at Jack.

"Now it just needs to cool for a bit!" I say over my shoulder, then start busying myself with the dishes.

Suddenly, Jack is next to me. Right next to me. "You wash, I dry?" he says, a dish towel in his hand.

"Yep!" I say. Why are my hands still shaking?

Jack and I don't talk as we do dishes, and I just tell myself it's because we're making so much noise, but I wonder if he's thinking about when my finger jabbed his chest, too. I wonder if he's thinking about how close we're standing to each other now. If he can feel the warmth from my body the way I can feel the warmth from his. If the way his hand brushes against mine when he takes dishes from me sends jolts of electricity through his body the way it's sending them through mine.

Jack dries the last mixing bowl, then slings the towel over his shoulder and leans against the sink. I turn the water off and join him. It's very quiet in the kitchen. Jack and I are still standing very close to each other.

"Think the pie is ready?" He turns his head toward me just a little, so he's looking at me out of the corner of his eye, almost like he's nervous to make eye contact with me or something, which I know is ridiculous. Jack Harper is way too confident, way too . . . everything to get nervous.

I notice I'm looking at him the same way, though, from the corner of my eye. So I can just see a hint of his long eyelashes, the slight stubble on his chin. Because I am too nervous to look right at him in this moment. Which is silly. So silly. I've spent the evening baking with him.

"Usually pie should cool for a few hours—"

"Hours!" Jack says, turning to face me. "You never mentioned that part!"

I turn, too, so we're facing each other directly again. He's got a slight pout to his bottom lip, and I can't tell if it's intentional. I find myself smiling. Not because his pouty lip is adorable. Definitely not. But because I'm amused by how badly he wants to try the pie.

"I mean, in an ideal world, the pie would chill for four hours." Jack's whole face turns into a pout, and I find myself laughing. "But this is a test kitchen of sorts, so I think we can try some now."

"Oh, thank goodness," Jack says.

He rummages through a drawer. It's both disorienting and comforting to see the ease with which he now moves around my kitchen. He pulls out a butter knife and lifts it above the pie.

I grab his hand. The warmth of it surprises me. "Jack, Jack, Jack," I say, "allow me to introduce you to a friend of mine. Her name is pie cutter."

"Kinda like pie—" he starts, but stops when he sees the look on my face.

I ignore the reference to my nickname and say, "Oh, you have so much to learn." I gently, carefully cut the pie. It could definitely use more time to cool, but I also can't deny either of us the deliciousness of a warm piece of pie.

I slide a piece onto a plate and hand him a fork. And just like with the pecan pie that fateful afternoon at Cup o' Jo, he starts inhaling it.

"This is so good," he says, his mouth stuffed with pie. "Thank you."

I can't help but laugh looking at him. And I can't help but feel proud, too.

"Don't forget your contributions," I remind him.

He laughs. "Yeah, can you imagine if I'd made the pie without your instructions?"

I think about his first attempt to measure cream. "No thanks."

"Are you some kind of wizard or witch?" he asks, his mouth still full. "How do you do this?"

"Remember that whole part where I showed you how to bake a pumpkin pie, with step-by-step directions?"

He laughs again. He takes a few more bites and then says, "You know, it just occurred to me. If this pie could be turned into a pumpkin spice latte, I bet it would sell really well at Cup o' Jo."

"Yeah, I'll just stick it in a blender," I say sarcastically.

"I'm serious!" Jack persists.

"About putting the pie in a blender?" I ask.

Jack smirks at me. "No, the taste, the spices. It all tastes like a pumpkin spice latte," he goes on, ignoring me. He takes another bite of pie, chews thoughtfully.

"But surely not better than the sacred, beloved Java Junction pumpkin spice latte?" I ask, unable to keep the sarcasm out of my voice.

Jack takes another nibble. "Better than Java Junction's pumpkin spice latte."

I gasp, then realize he's kidding. He must be kidding. "Hilarious," I say.

"I'm not joking," he says in a serious voice.

"Well, maybe you should joke. You don't want your family to disown you for speaking such blasphemy."

"I think you guys should serve this pumpkin spice latte at Cup o' Jo."

"This pumpkin spice latte?" I say. "The one that currently exists in a solid state?"

"If you can make this into coffee form, it would blow Java Junction's pumpkin spice latte out of the water."

"And remind me again why this is something you want to happen?" I ask, looking at him skeptically.

"I dunno. I mean, I know my parents didn't set up shop across the street from you guys to hurt your business or anything, but I still worry—"

Suddenly, I'm mad. Really mad. "Listen, we don't need any help from you or Java Junction, okay? We don't need your sympathy, your help, your rescuing. Especially the last part. I do not need to be rescued by a dude."

"I'm not trying to rescue you!" Jack says, that hurt look creeping back onto his face again. "Help, just help."

"Help implies I need rescuing," I quickly shoot back.

Jack sighs again. "Listen, Lucy, I like you. I care about you."

There is that word again. *Care.* I think about my finger against his chest. I think about the warmth I felt emanating from his body when we did dishes together. But then I remember who he is. Who his parents are. The shop they own. How weird it is that he's in my kitchen, offering me business advice.

"I just think those pictures, your aesthetic, could really help your social media presence, and with this pie being so good, there is some serious potential to turn it into an awesome drink—"

"Wow, thank you for mansplaining to me how to make Cup o' Jo more profitable! Means a lot coming from someone who admitted he doesn't know the first thing about baking or cooking, and earlier admitted he doesn't understand the appeal of it."

Jack's face crumples. "I told you that stuff, because, because . . ."

If he says the confusing word *care* one more time . . .

But I decide to cut him to the chase. I think again about how I have to look at Java Junction every time I go to Cup o' Jo, a place that used to be a refuge, a comfort for me. My other home. I think about my stupid nickname at school that he started. I think about the dessert contest I lost, when he was a judge. I think about my mom's worried face, our slowing business. I think about all the unhappiness I've experienced since he entered my life. "You know what? I think you should just leave," I say. "Lesson over. You wanted to make a pie, we made a flipping pie."

Jack looks defeated, hurt, sad, a whole bunch of feelings that I don't want to figure out, because it's not up to me to sort his emotional needs. I have my own emotions to sort out. Which I will do on my own. Not with anyone else's help. Especially not his.

Jack nods. I follow him as he grabs his jacket from our front hall tree. He pauses at our front door, hand on the knob, like he wants to say something else, but he just shakes his head and leaves, closing the door behind him.

16

My baking lesson with Jack replays in my head all morning at school the next day. The warmth I felt from his body when I did dishes with him. The little jolts of electricity I felt when our hands touched. The goofy way he sang to the cream. Even the way he interacted with Pancakes.

And then I think about his *advice* about somehow turning my pumpkin pie into a pumpkin spice latte, like it's just that easy. The way he said he cared about me. But then also, how completely complicated and confusing my life has been since he entered it. How his parents' business decision is affecting my mom's business, and my mom. Can I really trust anything Jack Harper says or does? Can I trust anything about Jack Harper at all?

I'm so distracted that Ms. Goldsmith has to repeat her question about quadratic equations to me three times before I even hear her. When I finally give her my answer, it's wrong.

I'm the first one at our lunch table. Amber joins a few seconds later, slightly out of breath. "I know we should wait for Evie to get here, but you didn't respond to my texts last night and I'm dying to know! How was it?" she says quickly, trying to catch her breath.

But then she looks at me closely, and says, "Oh no, what happened?"

And I want to tell her I hate Jack Harper again, but I'm not sure if I do, and everything is so confusing, and then Evie is at the table, too, staring at me, and it's all too much.

"Can we not talk about it, please?" I plead.

"Talk about what?" Evie asks.

Amber says, "Oh, yeah, let's definitely not talk about Spanish class today. I heard there was an awful quiz?"

Evie says, "Yeah, pretty brutal."

Amber is still watching me as she says, "Thanks for the tip! I have Spanish after lunch!" She takes out her textbook and starts flipping through the book, then takes out her notebook, and we all spend the rest of lunch conjugating verbs. None of us says a peep about Jack Harper. Not even when he waves at me from his lunch table and I don't wave back.

In English class, I pretend that Jack Harper never existed. It's annoyingly hard to do, especially because he keeps trying to catch my eye. Not that I'm looking in his direction at all. Not that I'm noticing him or his existence at all.

I'm distracted at Cup o' Jo, too, and mix up two customers' orders. It's a mistake that might happen on a busy day, but it's not a busy day. It's another slow day.

Finally, during a particularly long lull between customers, my mom joins me at the registers and asks, "Are you okay?"

Danielle is wiping down the counters for the millionth time, and Sheva went home since we've been so quiet.

"I'm . . . I . . ." I don't know what I am anymore. "I'll be fine."

"You'll be fine in a few minutes? Hours? Days? What kind of time span are we talking here?"

I know she's joking around, trying to make me feel better, but I don't say anything back.

"Does your 'I'll be fine in a questionable amount of time' have anything to do with your baking lesson with Jack Harper yesterday?"

I sigh. "Yeah."

"So he's secretly gone to culinary school and is actually an incredible baker? Is that it?"

I laugh, thinking about Jack singing to the cup of cream. "He was a surprisingly good student. But then he started making suggestions about how we should handle our socials, which I know need some help. The part that really made me mad was when he came up with this ridiculous idea that if we somehow turn my pumpkin pie into a pumpkin spice latte, it'll be better than Java Junction's PSL."

I look at her, waiting for her to agree with me, that the idea is preposterous, but she looks thoughtful. "You know, I think I know what he means."

"What?!" I say so loudly that Danielle drops the rag she's cleaning with.

"If you can get the proportions right, I think it is totally, absolutely one-hundred-percent doable. Especially because I know you won't include any chemical additives." She winks at me after saying the last part.

"And how do you propose I make my pumpkin pie into a pumpkin spice latte?"

"You could always put it in a—" my mom starts.

"Do. Not. Say. The. Word. Blender."

She laughs, says, "Well, I think it could be a fun project. Experiment. But only if it's something you want to do!"

"Yeah, something like that," I say, rubbing my head. "Plus it could increase—"

"Do. Not. Say. The. Word. Business."

I laugh now.

"Do we want to talk about his other suggestion?" she asks.

"If you are referring to increasing our social media presence, then yes. But he gets no credit—that was not his idea."

"I've been thinking we should update it for a while now. But I didn't want to ask you. You already do enough for me. And you know how much I dislike spending time on social media."

"Mom! Don't be afraid to ask me for things," I say, lightly whacking her with a dishcloth.

"Yes, *Mom*," she says. "How about we take a look at it together later, after closing?"

"Sure," I say.

"But, Lucy," she starts, "if this is another one of your attempts to try to increase—"

"Do. Not. Say. The. Word. Business," I say, and this time she whacks me with the dishcloth.

After we close the shop, my mom and I go to the local Chinese restaurant. The owners know us, and our orders, and soon my mom and I are at the kitchen table, steamed dumplings and cold sesame noodles on our plates.

I wipe my hands on my napkin and open Cup o' Jo's social media account.

"Yikes," I say.

"Yeah," my mom says.

"Our last post was from sometime over the summer, when I posted about our air-conditioning not working," I say. "Probably not the best picture to have as our most recent post."

"Want to put up some pictures of our menu offerings? Of new desserts you've made?"

"Wow, so you do know how this stuff works," I tease. "I thought you were anti–social media?"

"How do you think I find the best deals on stewed prunes? And denture cream?"

"You're such a dork," I mutter, but I'm smiling.

"Coupons for arthritis medicine," she goes on, making me laugh now.

"Such a dork!" I say louder.

"Oh yes, deals for those experiencing hearing loss due to old age. Thank you for speaking up."

It feels good to laugh. It feels good to laugh with my mom.

I open my gallery of pictures on my phone and we look through the images together: Things we've baked, my mom holding a beautifully crafted cappuccino, the pie that I entered in the festival dessert contest.

"Oh, this one is great," she says when she sees the pictures I took of Evie's apples at the apple orchard.

"Thanks," I say.

I try to quickly skip through the pictures I took at my disastrous baking lesson with Jack, but my mom stops at one, a photo of the cookbook and spice jars arranged just so. "This one is great, too," she says.

"I think we should stick to things strictly related to the shop, don't you?" I say in a tight voice.

I can feel her looking at me, but I keep my eye on my phone, tapping at images. "How about these?" I show her the images I selected: the picture of my mom holding the cappuccino; a picture of the outside of the Cup o' Jo storefront, the mountain just visible in the background; a picture of my apple cider cupcakes and caramel apple frosting; and a picture of a maple latte.

"Perfect!" she says. "But I really think the one from our kitchen would work, too. Give some personality to Cup o' Jo. Show our origins, make us more personable."

"Okay, fine," I say impatiently, tapping the picture. "Ready?" I ask, my finger hovering over the post button on my phone.

She smiles, just like she does when she asks me that every morning before we open the shop. "Ready."

I hit post and then immediately put my phone down, then pick it up again a minute later.

My mom laughs. "People aren't going to—"

I spin my phone around, show her that the post has a few likes already. "Oh!" she says.

"They're only from Amber and Evie, but a start, right?" I say.

My mom is still looking at my phone. "Oh, looks like Jack Harper just liked it, too!" she says, her voice chipper.

I grab my phone from her and put it face down on the table.

When I'm working on my homework that night, I get a text from Amber.

Amber

> I'm here if you want to talk about the baking lesson.

Lucy

> Jack Harper cannot be trusted.

Amber

> Déjà vu.

Lucy

> I know. I'll tell you about it. Soon.

Amber

> Whenever. Or not at all. Your call.

Lucy

> After all.

Amber

Poet didn't know it.

Lucy

Amber

Speaking of poetry, or something, nice posts on Cup o' Jo's socials.

Lucy

☺ Thanks. Had to be done.

Amber

Nice work, kid.

17

When I wake up the next morning, I see that the post from my baking lesson with Jack has gotten a ton of likes. A picture with the cookbook and the spice jars—167 likes. It must be a coincidence. Nothing to do with Jack Harper at all.

But annoyingly, during another lull at Cup o' Jo that afternoon, I find myself thinking about Jack again. Not Jack. But what Jack said about turning my pumpkin pie into a pumpkin spice latte. How ridiculous of an idea it is. Completely and utterly ridiculous.

Because I already know how to make a pumpkin spice latte. It pains me every time a customer orders one now, but I do it. My mom and I even created our very own pumpkin spice blend. But I also know my PSL lacks . . . something. It could be better somehow. The problem is, I don't know what any of those somethings or somehows are. But I do know that Java Junction does. They have mastered the perfect pumpkin spice latte.

However, their drink is based on artificial flavors. Their drink contains no actual real pumpkin. I think again about Jack's words, how if I could just turn my pumpkin pie into a drink, it would be the perfect pumpkin spice latte. Well, maybe it's time to give it a try.

I head to our back storeroom, where we have tons of cans of pumpkin. Not pumpkin pie filling, either, but real, actual pumpkin.

My mom looks up from her account-keeping book when I come back carrying a can of pumpkin. "Is this part of your project?"

"Experiment," I say. "How to create the world's best pumpkin spice latte. Or, at least, one better than Java Junction's. Jack Harper has told me that all Java Junction desserts are made off-site. And we know how fake their pumpkin spice lattes are. So I have decided the perfect pumpkin spice latte needs . . . real pumpkin."

My mom sighs. "Okay, but again, only if this is something fun for you, and not because—"

"Yes, yes," I say impatiently, ready to get to work.

My mom goes back to her account-keeping book, and I try again to ignore the furrow in her brow as I start.

I open our jar of premade pumpkin pie spice and give it a sniff. I can smell the cinnamon, nutmeg, ginger, cloves, and allspice. I don't think the spices are the problem. Then I brew the espresso and heat the milk. As I pour the espresso into the cup, it occurs to me: I'm not sure when to add the pumpkin to the drink, or how much to use. Well, all part of the experiment.

I pour in a little bit of maple syrup, sprinkle in our pumpkin pie spice mix, and a little vanilla. Now seems as good a time as any, so I add about a tablespoon of pumpkin puree. I figure the hot beverage will dissolve the pumpkin. I froth the milk and add it to the cup, along with whipped cream and a final sprinkle of cinnamon.

I look at my work, satisfied. I snap a couple pictures. Then, I take a deep breath, pick up the mug, and take a small sip. The glob of pumpkin floats to my mouth, and my theory about dissolving pumpkin is not just false but also gross.

Okay, fine. It was my first experiment. Did I really think I'd nail it on my very first attempt?

I try again, brewing more espresso, heating more milk, this time adding the pumpkin to the warm milk. But I'm met with the same result. The glob of pumpkin is smaller this time, but the pumpkin still doesn't dissolve, and it's still pretty gross.

Hmm. This might be harder than I thought.

Sheva looks over from where she's standing at the register. "Ooh, is the mad scientist hard at work?"

"Something like that," I mumble distractedly. I wander to the back of the shop, thinking maybe some physical distance from the drink will somehow inspire me.

Devon Stern and Sarah Jay are at the shop working. I look at them, wondering what their version of a perfect pumpkin spice latte would be. What is anyone's perfect pumpkin spice latte?

Darn Jack Harper and his annoying-to-execute advice.

All afternoon, between customers, of which we don't have a ton, I keep trying smaller and smaller globs of pumpkin, until I'm down to one-eighth teaspoon of pumpkin, and still it floats into my mouth, undissolved and gross.

After my disappointing luck trying to create the perfect pumpkin spice latte, that night I turn my attention back to Cup o' Jo's socials. I post some more pictures: the one from the apple orchard the other day, my pumpkin pie, and my apple crumb cake muffins.

After I post, I notice that we have a lot more followers now.

I read some of the comments. I recognize a lot of the usernames: There's Natalie Kerr, a junior, who lives down the street from me, saying she likes my pictures; Loren Kelly, who is on Amber's soccer team, saying she loves my kitchen; Lisa O'Brien, one of my mom's childhood friends, saying my cupcakes look delicious; Nicole Sanders, one of Evie's cousins, saying she needs one of my mom's cappuccinos now.

And then, of course, there is Jayden Lochman, calling me Pieface.

But as I read further, I realize there are other comments, too, from usernames I don't recognize. People talking to one another, tagging one another. I read those comments, too:

Hey, Briar Glen could be a cute weekend place to check out? Could get coffee here?

Look at this coffee place! Coffee dream paradise? Let's go!

Looks like a cute town.

And then finally, the last comments I read:

Do you serve pumpkin spice lattes?

No pumpkin spice lattes? #missedopportunity

Whatever, the PSL is way overdone!

Apple cider cupcakes!

I'd like 50 of those maple lattes please.

The small surge of pride I felt before has gotten bigger. It's also mixed with something else now, too, though. I realize it's excitement. Sure, these people could all just be saying they want to check out Cup o' Jo and never actually make the trip, but still, it seems like something? And something is better than nothing.

18

On Saturday, my mom, Danielle, and I are at the coffee shop. It's late afternoon, almost closing time, and my mom had already told Sheva she could leave early. Sheva said it was fine, she needed to get caught up on things at home, but she said it with a strained smile that my mom either hadn't noticed or had chosen to ignore. We only have one customer, a tourist, who I think just wanted to use our bathroom but felt guilty and ended up hastily ordering a peppermint tea.

Despite it being nearly closing time, we usually have at least a handful of customers, and the three of us are each trying to keep busy.

"How do we feel about Slowdive's new album?" Danielle asks. She's making a new playlist for the shop, saying how tired she is of the music we've been playing. I wonder if she's tired of the music because of how much less business we've had in the shop lately, and how much louder it makes the music seem.

"Whatever you think," my mom says. She's by the registers, tapping around at the tablet. Judging by the appearance of that worry line again, I think she's looking at our sales.

I'm once again fiddling with my attempt at a new and improved pumpkin spice latte, this time using more of our pumpkin spice mix and blending the canned pumpkin before I add it to the drink. I've finally gotten the texture right, no more floating pumpkin chunks, but it's still missing something.

"All right!" my mom says suddenly, startling the man drinking his tea. "Lucy, how about a trip to Patty's Pumpkin Patch? We are overdue for some pumpkin carving and decorating."

"Today?" I ask. Usually we plan our trips weeks, or at least days, ahead of time.

"Yup!" my mom says. It's 4:55, and she flips the CLOSED sign on the door.

The man gulps down the rest of his tea and mumbles "thanks" before he hurries out the door.

"Danielle, can you handle closing up?" my mom asks.

Most evenings my mom is the one to close, so Danielle looks a little surprised, but says, "Sure, no problem."

"Great! Let's go, Lucy."

My mom and I walk home. It's not until we're on our street, passing the Funchions' house, where the three kids are jumping in a pile of freshly raked leaves, that either of us speaks.

"Any reason in particular that you wanted to go to the patch today?" I ask carefully.

"What do you mean? We go every year."

"Yeah, it just seems sort of . . . last minute?"

"Well, life is short!" my mom says, in a weird fake chipper voice.

"Okay," I say, having that sense of being underwater and looking up at the world around me again.

But when we get in the car, my mom asks, "Should we drive the long way or the short way?" and my normal life shifts back into focus again.

It's a question she's asked every year since I can remember—we've been going to the same pumpkin patch all my life—and I always say the long way. Always. Even though we could hop on the interstate and be there in five minutes, we always go for the twenty-minute drive, which takes us up and down winding hills, orange and red and yellow leaves falling in front of our windshield the whole way.

Today is no different. "The long way," I say, and soon we're twisting our way up and down hills, the late-afternoon sun making the changing leaves' colors even more vibrant.

When we get to Patty's, we wave at Heather, who has been

working at the patch my entire life, and then start strolling among the rows of pumpkins.

"What kind of pumpkin vibe are you feeling this year?" my mom asks. "Think you'll want to paint it, or make a jack-o'-lantern?"

"Carving, definitely."

I look among the pumpkins, in every shape and size, in all shades of orange. I even see a few white pumpkins, and even one that's almost up to my knees. "How about that one?" I joke, pointing.

My mom seems startled. "That may be out of our price range."

"Mom, I was totally kidding," I say. "But what do you mean 'out of our price range'?"

"Nothing, nothing!" she answers quickly. "My attempt at a joke."

"Is it because of Java—"

"Lucy!" my mom says, a bit sharply. "I told you, it was just a joke."

We look at each other just a second longer, and I see the worry crease on her forehead.

"Let's keep looking!" she exclaims.

I trail behind her and spot a lopsided pumpkin with a small dent in the back. I know the "damaged" pumpkins cost less. "How about this one?"

She turns and wrinkles her nose. "You're still joking, right?"

"What? No!" I say. "Look at this poor defenseless pumpkin. It's like the Charlie Brown Christmas tree of pumpkins. I bet all it needs is some love and it'll clean up beautifully."

My mom looks at me skeptically. "Okay, if you're sure that's the one you want."

"Super sure!"

"Let's walk a little more, though, okay?"

Does she want to talk to me about something? Is she going to tell me more about Cup o' Jo financial stuff?

"Because it's a nice day, and it's nice to spend time with you," she says, as if reading my mind. She turns to face me, then touches my wool beanie, straightening it.

"Mom," I say, "you don't need to fix my hat."

She laughs. "Sorry! Old habits die hard." We're walking again. "I just remember when you were that big." She points to a baby in overalls who is sitting in her mom's lap, having her picture taken amid the pumpkins.

"Well, I don't," I say. "But I don't ever get tired of you telling me how cute I was!"

She nudges her shoulder against mine. "You were the cutest, smiliest baby ever. You loved naps. You really didn't like bananas for some reason. Every time I'd give you a piece—"

"I'd throw it on the ground." She's told me all this before, but I wasn't kidding; I really do love hearing about what I was like as a baby.

"And now look at you, working with me at Cup o' Jo," she says, still looking at the baby.

"When do I get promoted to manager?"

My mom looks at me. "Very funny."

"I mean, I'm not entirely kidding, I guess," I realize, as I start talking. "Like, when I'm in college, I can still live at home because it'll be a lot cheaper and so I can help at the shop—"

My mom puts her arm around me. "Lucy, we don't need to talk about this now."

"Well, why not?" I ask, feeling exasperated.

"Because you're sixteen! I want you to enjoy yourself. You don't need to think about college and where you'll live just yet. Take it from an old lady like me: You're only young once."

"But I want to keep working at Cup o' Jo," I insist.

My mom is quiet for a moment, her arm still around me. "I just want you to want it for the right reasons."

"What do you mean?"

"I want you to want to work at Cup o' Jo because you want to."

"That was a lot of wants."

"I'm serious, honey. I want you to work there, to follow in my footsteps if it's what you want. Not because it's something you feel you have to do."

"Of *course* I want to *want* to . . ."

"All right, end of lecture," my mom says. "Let's go pay for our Charlie Brown pumpkin."

We head into the farm store, strolling the aisles, which sell things like locally made apple butter, pumpkin butter, fresh fudge, local honey, little signs declaring one's love of fall.

When we reach the local produce section, my mom picks up a little gourd and examines it. Then she picks up a couple smaller pumpkins. "I want to make some soup with these guys. Speaking of, how is your pumpkin spice latte experiment coming along?"

"Ugh, it's coming. The latte is getting there, but I still feel like it's missing something," I say as I shift the pumpkin in my arms. Then it hits me.

"Pepitas!" I say so loudly some of the other shoppers turn to look at me.

My mom looks at me strangely, too. "Yes, honey, we can roast some pumpkin seeds."

"No, I think that's it!"

"What is it?" she asks, looking confused.

"I think that's what could make the drink better. Pepitas!"

My mom smiles. "That's a great idea! What kind of seasoning will you use on the pepitas? Pumpkin spice?"

"Mom!"

"I'm serious! Not about the pumpkin spice. But think about all the things you could season the seeds with. Nutmeg, cinnamon, maybe some cloves. And are you going to blend the seeds into a powder? What will—"

"Let's buy these pumpkins first, okay?" I say impatiently, eager to get to work.

When we get home, my mom puts down newspapers and takes out some kitchen knives.

"It's so nice that we can do something that has absolutely nothing to do with work!" As she says this last part, she's jabbing the knife into the area around the pumpkin stem, somewhat forcefully. She removes the knife and puts it in the sink, then wipes her forehead.

I'm still just standing there, watching her. "Mom are you—"

"Never better!" she says. "Let's make this jack-o'-lantern. You're not the only one curious about pumpkin seeds in a pumpkin spice latte."

She and I work in silence for a while, both of us concentrating on separating the seeds and putting them in a colander.

"Why do jack-o'-lanterns have to be called jack-o'-lanterns?" I mutter as I scoop the guts out of the pumpkin.

My mom laughs. "If you want to talk about the baking lesson—"

"Nope!" I say quickly.

My mom says, "Okay. But if you change your mind—"

"Yep!"

"Okay, got it," she says, knowing that pressing me for details will get me nowhere except mad.

We're quiet again.

"How are you going to get pepitas into the coffee?" my mom asks.

"Mortar and pestle? Or maybe a food processor?" I start to wonder if this is another bad idea. "Do you think that will make the drink too powdery? Like hot chocolate made from a mix, but the powder isn't dissolved correctly?"

She shrugs. "I don't know. But what if you used real pumpkin puree, from a real pumpkin?"

I look at the pumpkin guts scattered around us.

My mom laughs. "Not from *this* pumpkin—from a sugar pumpkin. One you roast in the oven. Like the ones I just bought to make soup."

"You really think fresh pumpkin is that much different than canned pumpkin?" I ask skeptically.

"Think about peaches in the summertime—how ripe and juicy they are. Think about our peach cobbler."

"I think I might be drooling a little bit."

"Now think about canned peaches," she says. "Imagine using those in the cobbler."

Suddenly, my mouth is drier. "Mom . . . that's actually an incredible idea!" I'm starting to feel really excited. "That could be *exactly* what I need! Fresh pumpkin could change everything!"

"Slow down, Lucy," my mom says. "I was just thinking out loud. We won't know how the drink is until you try it with the new ingredients."

But I barely hear her. I'm too busy rinsing one of the sugar pumpkins.

"Hey! I was going to use those for soup," my mom says.

I turn around, holding the pumpkin, and give her a pleading look.

She sighs. "But I can always get another one."

I pick up a knife, and my mom grabs it from me. "At least let me handle this part?" she says as she cuts the area around the stem off, then cuts the pumpkin in half.

I get to work scooping out more pumpkin guts, adding more pumpkin seeds to our colander. I look up, and my mom is still working on our bigger pumpkin.

"Our jack-o'-lantern!" I say. "We need to finish it! What kind of face are we thinking this year?"

"Lucy, it's okay. We can finish it while you're roasting those other pumpkins."

Still, I feel a little guilty as I clean out my pumpkin. My mom wanted to carve pumpkins to keep her mind off the shop, and I've brought her right back to Cup o' Jo.

I preheat the oven, brush some olive oil on the pumpkins, and stick them in the oven. As my mom and I carve the angriest jack-o'-lantern I ever remember carving, the house fills with the smell of roasting pumpkin.

I can barely contain my excitement as I peel the skin off the pumpkin and put the rest of the pumpkin into the food processor. I give it a few pulses, and soon I have a pumpkin puree that looks nothing like the canned stuff I've been using. I take out two spoons, handing one to my mom.

"Ready?" she asks me.

"Ready."

And we sample the most delicious pumpkin puree I've ever tasted.

"Mom, you are a genius," I say, hugging her.

She puts her hands up. "We still don't know if this is the solution!"

"I can't wait until tomorrow morning to find out!"

I start brewing an espresso, then pour it into a mug, sprinkle in our homemade pumpkin spice mix, and add maple syrup and vanilla. I quickly froth the milk. Then, the moment of truth. I add two tablespoons of my fresh puree to the drink and stir. This time, the pumpkin completely dissolves! I finish with whipped cream and a sprinkle of cinnamon.

"This is it, Mom! This has to be it!"

"Lucy, we don't know—"

I take a sip before she can finish her sentence. The drink is good. Really good. But . . . it's still missing something.

"This isn't it," I say, handing the drink to my mom.

She takes a small, thoughtful sip. "I think it might be?"

"No," I say stubbornly. "It's still missing something! What the heck could it possibly be missing?"

"Honey, it's a delicious drink. I didn't want this taking over your life, and I'm afraid that's exactly what has happened."

There is a small part of me that knows she's right. But there's an even bigger part of me that knows I can make this drink better.

I *will* make this drink better.

19

Lucy

Hypothetically speaking, if you were going to make a pumpkin spice latte with real pumpkin puree, but it still tasted like it was missing something, what would you add?

Evie

Who are you and what have you done with Lucy? The Lucy I know strongly dislikes pumpkin spice lattes.

Lucy

Strongly dislikes is too strong.

Evie

Like I said, who are you, and what have you done with Lucy?

Lucy

I'm trying to create the perfect PSL.

Our socials are doing well. But we're still slow. The people want PSLs.

Amber

I've seen all your posts! Nice work, friend.

Lucy

Thanks, friend. Was so overdue, though.

Evie

Been saying that forever.

Lucy

Amber

Your PSL is good already!

Lucy

I know. And I made an even better one with my mom using real pumpkin. But I still want better. The best.

Evie

Better than Java Junction? Like just come out and say it?

Lucy

FINE. I'm trying to make a better PSL than Java Junction. But there is a reason theirs is the best, because making one without artificial ingredients is impossible!

Evie

I could have told you that.

Lucy

Super helpful.

Amber

You used fresh pumpkin?

Lucy

Yes. I thought it was the perfect solution! Canned pumpkin is gross.

Evie

And?

Lucy

And what?

Evie

And what else have you tried?

Lucy

That's it so far.

Amber

You spend weeks tweaking ingredients until you get the perfect dessert. Might take a few tries to get the perfect drink?

Lucy

I don't have a few tries! It's almost Halloween! People want to have this mythical perfect PSL at Cup o' Jo.

Amber

Do you think maybe you're putting a smidge too much pressure on yourself?

Lucy

A smidge. Seriously?

Evie

??

Amber

??

Lucy

Nothing. Jack Harper told me I should turn my pumpkin pie into a PSL!

Evie

Still not following . . . a smidge?

Lucy

NEVER MIND. Maybe I'll just stick a piece of pumpkin pie in the blender and splash in some coffee.

Evie

Now you're talking!

Amber

It's cool that you're updating Cup o' Jo's socials. But I don't think you need to create the perfect drink for some internet strangers who might visit Briar Glen.

Evie

What about different spices? Something you haven't tried before? Something surprising?

Lucy

Maybe that's it? I'm being too obvious. I need some kind of surprise spice! Something no one would ever expect to find in their PSL. Evie, you are a genius!

Evie

Um, thanks and you're welcome, I guess?

Lucy

BRB!

Lucy

Okay that didn't go so well. Rosewater and cinnamon. Honey and coriander seeds. Do not recommend.

Amber

Don't give up yet!

Lucy

Who said anything about giving up?

Evie

You know who might have some ideas?

Lucy

Do not say his name. I don't even want to see it on my screen.

Amber

The baking lesson was that bad, huh?

Lucy

Yes and no. It's complicated.

Evie

Good complicated or bad complicated?

Lucy

Is there ever a good complicated?

Evie

I think complications are usually necessary plot points to most dramatic movies.

Lucy

I don't want a dramatic movie. I just want the perfect PSL.

Evie

Well, maybe you don't need to look that far.

Lucy

The PSL is within me?

Evie

Something like that. Or you could just ask someone if they have any tips.

Lucy

No way. Plus, there is that whole thing with us having competing businesses?

Amber

You're not asking for the recipe. Just tips. Desperate times.

Lucy

These are not desperate times.

That night, I toss and turn, mentally putting together different spices. The thing is, though, I've always thought our spice blend was perfect. Ginger, nutmeg, cinnamon, cloves, and allspice. I truly can't think of a more perfect combination.

Around four a.m., I get out of bed and head down to the kitchen for a glass of water.

My mom is at the table, her laptop open. Her back is to me, but I can see she's looking through her financial spreadsheets. Then she puts her head down, and I hear her start to cry. For a moment, I consider asking her what's wrong, if she wants to talk—but I know the answers to both questions, and my presence would only make things worse. So I go back to my room, more determined than ever to make the perfect pumpkin spice latte.

For my mom.

20

"Things might be getting a little desperate," I say quietly to Amber and Evie at lunch. Thinking about my mom makes my eyes well up, but I refuse to cry.

"Are you okay?" Amber asks. "What happened?"

"Nothing!" I snap. Then, in a gentler voice, "I saw my mom looking at money stuff for the shop. It doesn't seem good."

Amber looks like she wants to say something, but even if she is my best friend, I still don't want her sympathy.

I go on, "So maybe asking Jack if he has any pumpkin spice latte tips might not be the worst idea in the world."

She looks at me, eyebrow raised, waiting for me to say more.

"It could also end up being the worst idea in the world," I add.

Evie shrugs. "Don't know until you try?"

"Thanks for the reassurance!" I say sarcastically.

"Did I ever promise reassurance in the terms of our friendship?" she asks. "I think honesty is more my thing."

I sigh and look at Jack's table. He's just sat down and is talking to his friends. "Well, here goes nothing. Or everything."

"Godspeed," Evie says.

Jack stops his conversation with his friends when I approach his table. He gestures to the empty seat across from him.

"Sorry to interrupt," I say as I sit down. "I want to talk to you about something."

"You're not interrupting anything," Jack says in his easy way.

And it's true; the guys at his table don't even seem to notice me as they talk about their upcoming soccer game.

"So what's up?"

"Well, first, I wanted to apologize."

"You do?" Jack says, looking surprised.

I pick at the edge of the table, unable to meet his gaze. "I'm sorry for the way our baking lesson ended the other day. Especially when you were just trying to help."

Jack looks confused. "No, I'm sorry. I was being nosy. And, actually, I wanted to thank you."

"Why?"

"Thank you for helping me learn how to measure a cup of cream! How to make a pie! How to cut a pie," he says, ticking off the reasons on his fingers.

"Oh, you're welcome," I say. "But I'm still sorry."

"I'm sorry, too," he says.

We look at each other for a second.

"You said there was something you wanted to talk to me about?" Jack asks, breaking the silence.

I close my eyes and take a deep breath. I think about my mom crying at the table, how I'd do anything in the world for Cup o' Jo. Anything for my mom. I open my eyes and see that Jack is looking at me curiously. "Remember when you said that thing about turning my pumpkin pie into a pumpkin spice latte?"

Jack looks at me in confusion.

I press on. "At the baking lesson. You said that thing about how if my pumpkin pie could be turned into a pumpkin spice latte, it might be a really good drink?"

Recognition flashes across Jack's face. "Yeah . . ."

"Okay, so maybe it's not the worst idea in the world."

Jack has a little smile on his lips, and for some annoying reason, a reflex in my brain decides I should smile back. I try to make my face stop smiling, but it can't. It's like trying to hold back a sneeze, so I try to focus on my mission. *Think about Mom, about Cup o' Jo.*

"Wait a second, are you saying I was right about something?" He puts his hands on the sides of his face, feigning shock.

I sigh. "Yes. No. Maybe."

He laughs, and his laugh is as frustratingly contagious as his smile.

"Lucy Kane, are you saying you need my help with something?"

"No!" I say quickly. "Maybe. I maybe might appreciate any suggestions you might have on how one might turn a pie into a delicious drink. A delicious *autumnal* drink."

"Well, when you put it that way . . ."

"I know it's, like, a conflict of interest for you to even help, given your whole Java Junction thing."

"My whole 'Java Junction thing,'" he says, laughing. "That ol' thing. Well, I just see it as giving advice."

"Do you have any idea how much I don't want to ask for your help?"

"Lucy, I'll help you. *Try* to help you. Okay? I guess I'm confused why you're asking me, and why you're asking me now."

I really don't want to get into it. "Listen, forget I asked, okay?"

"I was about to say, it's none of my business," he says quietly. "But if I can help you in any way, I'd be happy to."

"And?"

"And what?" He's still confused.

"I don't know." I feel confused myself. "I guess . . . are you wondering what you get out of the deal, or something?"

"Lucy, not everything has to be a business transaction, okay?

Sometimes people want to help people, or try to at least, just because. No strings attached," Jack says. "After our lesson, I watched some YouTube videos about baking. And about different kinds of flavored coffees. The history of some seasonal beverages—"

"Okay, now I *know* you're just messing with me."

"I'm not!" he says, laughing that same contagious laugh again. "I felt kinda like a doofus after our lesson, realizing how clueless I am when it comes to baking, or anything cooking- or kitchen-related at all, and like, especially with my parents' careers, and them owning a few Java Junctions—"

I find myself automatically groaning when I hear the name, then look at Jack, wondering if he heard me.

If he did, he decides to ignore me, because he goes on, "Anyway, I guess you were kinda an inspiration? It's really cool how much you know about your mom's business, how involved you are with Cup o' Jo, and it made me want to be . . . better?"

Did Jack Harper just call me an inspiration?

"Thanks?" I say, feeling even more confused.

"Anyway, like I said, I don't know how much help I'll be, but I feel like I owe you. We'll call it . . ."—he's thinking—"the Great Pumpkin Spice Latte Creation Project!"

I laugh. "A bit wordy, don't you think?"

"Perhaps. Anyway, we can figure out the name later. When

should our crafting begin? Our creating?" He rubs his hands together, a bit like an evil scientist.

"How about tomorrow afternoon? I'm done at Cup o' Jo around five."

"Perfect!" he says. "My place this time?"

I think for a second. Suddenly, I'm very, *very* curious about what his house is like.

"Yeah, okay," I say hesitantly.

"Perfect!" he says. "I'll text you the address right now."

I look at the address, and I'm surprised. He's on the other end of town, in one of the quietest sections.

"What?" he asks, noticing the surprise on my face.

"Nothing," I say quickly.

There is one "high-rise" building in all of Briar Glen, and most locals hate it. It's not even much of a high-rise, just a six-story building compared to the usual two- or three-story buildings on Briar Glen's Main Street, but it's a building that many people mention with disdain. I had assumed that's where Jack's family lived. Or where the owners of a Java Junction would live.

Jack looks unconvinced but says, "See you tomorrow?"

"See you tomorrow," I reply. As I walk back to my table, I wonder what other surprises Jack Harper is hiding.

21

The next day at school somehow flies by, and I spend a lot of my shift at Cup o' Jo fiddling with and adding pictures to our account, reading through comments from people, now almost entirely from accounts I don't recognize:

Perfect fall weekend destination.

We're going this weekend!

Can't wait to try your coffee!

I'm busy posting a few pictures from the fall festival when I say to my mom, "I'm going to go to Jack Harper's house after my shift today."

My mom stops wiping down the counter. "I'm sorry, it almost sounds like you said you're going to Jack Harper's house?"

"Err, may I go to Jack Harper's house?"

"Yes, you may, but obviously you need to tell me why," she says. "I thought the two of you didn't get along?"

"We don't," I say. "I just thought he might have some tips on making a pumpkin spice latte."

She wrinkles her nose. "You think that's a good idea, taking drink advice from our competition?"

"I thought Java Junction wasn't our competition."

"Not competition, you're right," she says, correcting herself. "But I wouldn't exactly call them our business allies, either."

"I know. It's weird," I say. "I just want to get this drink right. Everyone online is pretty much begging us for one, and all these people are talking about coming to Cup o' Jo. If we can make the perfect pumpkin spice latte, then it'll really help business."

My mom sighs. "Honey, I told you, we're doing okay, financially. And I also told you to stop worrying about that kind of stuff!"

She's lying to me. But I can't think about that now. I can't. "I know, I know," I say. "It just seems like a missed opportunity. We can do better."

My mom looks at me quietly for a second. "I told you, don't spend too much more time thinking about it or experimenting, okay? You give enough of yourself to this place as it is."

"Yeah, because I love this place."

"I know you do, honey. But I just don't want you to forget to be a teenager, too. You have the rest of your life to be a grown-up. Trust me, it's not nearly as exciting as it looks."

"So is it okay if I go to Jack's?"

"It is, but promise to actually, maybe, have fun, okay?"

"I don't like to make promises I can't keep," I say. "But I'll try."

An hour later, I'm standing outside Jack's house. It's a bungalow on a quiet treelined street. I take a deep breath and ring the bell.

Jack's dad opens the door.

"Hi, Mr. Harper," I say.

"Hi, Lucy," he responds, opening the front door wider so I can come in, like me hanging out with his son is just totally normal.

"Jack's in the kitchen. He wouldn't tell me what you guys were up to exactly, just some kind of kitchen experiment?" He shrugs. "I told him he can do whatever he wants, just please don't burn the place down."

I laugh. "Deal. I won't burn your place down."

He laughs, too. "The kitchen is just back there, behind the dining room," he says, gesturing.

"Thank you," I say, heading in the direction he's pointing.

Jack is in the kitchen, rummaging through cabinets, pulling out spice jars and putting them on the counter. He stops when he sees me and smiles. "You ready for phase one of the Great Pumpkin Spice Latte Creation Project?"

"Phase one? How many phases do you think we'll need?"

"As many as it takes."

I groan. "You do realize fall is, like, a finite season, right? Halloween is just around the corner! And then people are going to be moving on to peppermint lattes."

"All the more reason to get started now!" Jack says. "So, my question for you: What have you tried so far?"

"Good news!" I say. "Turns out pumpkin spice lattes made with real pumpkin are actually pretty good." I show him the jar of pumpkin puree my mom and I made the other day.

"Okay, then what's the problem?"

"I don't know. The drink still needs something more."

"More pizazz?" he offers.

"You and your vocabulary," I mutter.

"What does your pumpkin spice latte taste like, anyway? I've never had one since you so cruelly denied me the one time I asked, remember?"

"If this is a reference to me throwing a pie—"

"It's not!" he says quickly, hands up in surrender.

I sigh. "Fine. I need to make one, anyway, to show you what I'm working with. Can you brew some espresso?" I ask as I pull more of my supplies out of my tote bag.

Jack looks at me blankly.

I point to the fancy espresso machine on his counter.

"I don't really know how to use it?" he admits sheepishly.

I look at him for a second. "Well, I'm not giving you espresso-making lessons today!"

I quickly brew a shot, then add the pumpkin puree, our spice mix, and vanilla. His espresso machine has its own frother, so I pour the frothed milk on top. I pull whipped cream out of my tote, then the cinnamon, and then the drink is ready.

Jack watches this all, wordlessly.

"Here you go," I say, handing him the drink.

"How did you do that so fast?"

I ignore his question. "Just try the drink. Please tell me what it's missing!"

He eagerly takes the mug, gently blows on it, and then takes a small sip.

"You don't need to say anything. I know. It's not that great."

"No, it's good," Jack says quickly.

I don't want to say he looks disappointed, but he does look slightly baffled.

"But?"

"But . . ." He takes another sip. "I know what you mean. I feel like it's missing something?" I can tell he's choosing his words carefully.

"We can't all make a perfect pumpkin spice latte like Java Junction."

"No, I'm not comparing. It's just that, yeah, after having your pumpkin pie, which was so good, it just feels like this drink is missing . . . some—"

"So what do you think it's missing?" It comes out in a snarky tone of voice.

"More spices?"

"Which ones? I've already tried more cinnamon, more nutmeg. It's still just missing something."

"What about cloves?" Jack suggests.

"I've already got a tiny bit of cloves in there."

"Well, what if you add more?"

And before I can say anything else, Jack opens a jar of cloves, adds two teaspoons to my latte, and gives it a quick stir. "There!" he says, clearly satisfied with his work.

"I've never put that many cloves in anything I've ever made."

"All the more reason I added extra! It'll be a pumpkin spice latte like we've never had before!"

"That's for sure," I say under my breath.

"Give it a try!" he says, handing me the cup.

"Me?" I say. "Why do I have to be the guinea pig?"

"What, you don't trust me?"

I peer into the cup. It's a weird color. Almost auburn. It should look pretty, but something about it looks odd.

"You have no faith!" Jack says, taking the cup out of my hands. But he doesn't take a sip.

"Uh-huh," I say, crossing my arms. "Who has no faith, again?"

He sniffs the drink apprehensively. "Did I put too many cloves in there?"

"You tell me," I say, smiling despite myself.

We both peer into the cup at the same time, and when we look up, our faces are a few inches apart. I jump back. "Wow, that's a stinky drink!" I say, waving my hand in front of my nose, trying to recover.

"Fragrant, for sure," Jack concurs, also waving his hand in front of his nose. "Okay, this is silly! How are we ever going to make the best pumpkin spice latte if we don't sample our recipes, right? And adding the extra cloves was my idea, so here goes nothing!" And in one quick motion he takes a gulp of the drink . . . and promptly runs over to the sink to spit it out.

He turns the faucet on and cups his hands under the water and starts gulping from his cupped hands. Jack finally turns back to me, water dripping down his chin.

"That good, huh?" I ask.

Wordlessly he opens the fridge and pulls out a slice of cheese, which he immediately stuffs in his mouth. He chews quickly, grabs a glass from the cabinet, and fills it with water. It occurs to me how weird it is to watch him move around his kitchen. That I'm in his kitchen right now. But I'm too distracted by his reaction to the drink to think about it for very long.

He chugs the glass of water and looks at me, his eyes watering. "I feel like I just drank liquid potpourri."

I can't help it; I start to smile a little bit.

He crosses his arms. "I'm so glad that my pain and misery are funny to you."

"I'm sorry!" I say, trying to make my face serious.

But the more I try, the harder it is, and I just feel my smile getting bigger, until I'm full-blown laughing, and Jack is, too.

Finally, he says, "Okay, back to the drawing board," looking slightly disappointed now.

"Did you just expect the first drink to be perfect?"

"No, of course not. I guess I just thought it'd be . . . easier?"

"Ah, because things aren't ever hard for Jack Harper." I say it in a teasing voice, but I realize I mean it.

"What does that mean?" Jack asks.

"Are things ever a struggle for you? Like . . . do things ever not come naturally to you?"

"Remember that whole baking thing, how terrible I was at it?"

"Yeah, and then you figured it out, and now you're helping me, and . . ." I pause. "Are you a robot? Like, are there cogs and wheels in there?" I touch his forehead, then immediately pull my hand away.

"Lucy Kane? What on earth are you talking about?" he asks, laughing, looking at my hand.

I sigh. "Okay, it's going to sound ridiculous, but when you first moved to Briar Glen, I kinda thought you might have been a robot. I mean, not really, but yeah, maybe also a little bit?"

"Yeah, you're going to have to tell me what the heck you're talking about," he says, tearing his eyes away from my hand, looking into my eyes, still laughing.

"You're just so, like . . . perfect," I say. "You moved to Briar Glen, and you immediately fit in, like it was just so effortless for you. You're obviously the best student in English class, and you were immediately popular, like, even becoming instant friends with Melanie Craddock and half the soccer team. Who does that?"

He shrugs. "Someone who's had to move a lot?"

"I'm sorry," I say quietly.

"I'm going to tell you something." He looks at me earnestly. "I can't believe I'm telling you this, but I am. Okay." He takes a deep breath. "The first time we moved, when I was six, I peed my pants on my first day of first grade at my new school. Like, legit had an accident in the middle of gym class."

"What?" I say, laughing hysterically. I'm picturing a mini Jack Harper, with wet pants, and it's so cute, but so sad.

He cracks a little smile. "It's finally kinda funny now, ten years later, but at the time, I felt like my life was over. And do you know why it happened?"

"I think I understand how kidneys function and need to have the waste removed."

His eyes open in horror, and now it's even easier to picture a little Jack, scared, and suddenly I stop laughing.

"I had an accident because I was too nervous—too shy—to ask where the bathroom was."

"Oh," I say quietly.

"I know! It's so embarrassing, and I can't believe I actually just told you all that. Anyway, of course no one could let me forget it. I was teased every day for the two years we lived in San Francisco."

"And then what happened?"

"Then we moved. And we moved again. And we moved again. And I won't say that each move got easier, because it didn't. I think each move was harder. Because the older I got, the more engrained, already established, the friendships were with each new place. The more history there was between people. It's why I read so much. Sometimes it's nice to escape to a different world when mine keeps changing. But at some point, I decided I could either be an outsider or I could just . . ."

"Become a robot?" I offer softly.

He makes a face at me. "I didn't want to be a spectator. To my own life, you know? I just wanted to live it, be in it, so I did."

"You make it sound so easy."

"It's not. But it's better than the alternative. Never living my life, always just watching. So don't be like me. Don't be afraid to ask where the bathroom is."

"Don't be afraid to ask where the bathroom is," I repeat, in a daze.

He laughs.

"I've never lived anywhere but Briar Glen," I say.

"And that's awesome! You've grown up with so many of these

people, have known so many of them your entire life."

I pause, considering. "Yeah, I guess. Except when they know way too many things about me. Like anything and everything I've ever done, chances are someone remembers it. That's why I was so upset about the nickname, because—"

"I still swear it wasn't me!" Jack says quickly.

"Oh, I wasn't trying to start that conversation again. I just meant the nickname is the kind of thing that can follow you around forever when you live in a town like Briar Glen, with people you have known your entire life."

"It must be cool, though, in some ways? Like, you're part of this huge family. You get on each other's nerves and drive each other crazy, but ultimately, you all really do care about each other."

"I never really thought of it that way before," I say. I'm quiet for a second. "What if I can't live anywhere but Briar Glen? Like, what if I can't exist anywhere else?"

"Of course you can."

"That's easy for you to say."

"So, what, you just stay in Briar Glen the rest of your life?"

"I mean, I could," I say hesitantly.

"You could, yeah. But you could also do anything you want."

"What do you mean, 'anything I want'?"

"I mean, Lucy, you're smart; you already have more business skills than a lot of grown-ups I know. You know how to bake. I don't think you realize how talented you are. You're creative. You could do anything you want."

I feel my face flushing. "That's really nice of you to say all that stuff," I'm speaking quietly.

"I'm not saying it to be nice. I'm saying it because it's true."

"Thank you," I say, not quite able to meet his gaze.

"Do you *want* to stay in Briar Glen for the rest of your life?"

"I kinda always thought I would, in some ways. I could still live at home when I go to college, keep helping my mom at the shop."

"I doubt your mom would let you stay in Briar Glen the rest of your life."

"But she needs me. Who else could help her in the shop? I know everything there is to know about Cup o' Jo, what it takes to run it."

"I don't doubt that. But she also needs you to go out and live your life."

"I do live my life!" I insist. But then I think of all the weekends I've spent at Cup o' Jo. The time I've spent updating our social media and trying to create the perfect pumpkin spice latte. "But I shouldn't be a spectator," I say softly.

"What?"

"Don't be a spectator, and don't be afraid to ask where the bathroom is," I say, in a bit of a daze.

He laughs. "Something like that, yeah."

"See, you even give perfect advice," I say. "Are you sure you're not a robot?" I put out my hand to touch his forehead again, then quickly let it fall.

He looks at my hand, then picks it up in his own. His hand is warm, the skin soft. "I promise," he says. He links his pinkie with mine. "Pinkie promise."

We stand there, hand in hand, pinkie fingers intertwined, looking at each other, but then suddenly I hear the front door opening, Jack's mom's voice calling his name, and we both let go of each other's hands like we were about to burn them on something.

Maybe we were.

When I get home that night, I text Amber and Evie.

Lucy

So I don't have the perfect PSL yet. But I might understand Jack a little better.

Evie

And he's not a terrible human being?

Lucy

Perhaps not.

Amber

Is it too soon to tell you I told you so?

Lucy

Yes.

Amber

Just checking.

22

Jack insists we attempt another latte a few days later, and I'm not about to argue. It's almost the weekend, and October is quickly zipping by, and the window of opportunities I have to make the perfect pumpkin spice latte is rapidly closing.

Jack comes to my house this time. Pancakes eagerly greets him and immediately begins purring as Jack takes off his coat.

"Okay, I've been doing some more brainstorming," he says as he bends to pet the purring cat.

"You have?" I ask. I'm both surprised and touched.

"Of course I have!" he says, standing up with Pancakes in his arms. "I think our proportions are off."

"How do you figure?" I ask skeptically.

"I think we need more cream." He's still looking at my cat. "Don't you agree, Pancakes?"

Pancakes is now doing what my mom and I call her exploding purr and is half-dozing in Jack's arms.

"More cream?"

"Yes, more cream of the whipped variety," Jack says, scratching Pancakes behind the ears.

I walk into the kitchen, Jack and Pancakes behind me. Jack finally puts her down in the window seat.

"There is already a lot of whipped cream in my pumpkin spice latte," I say.

"I think we should try more."

"Seriously?"

"Seriously," he says. "Allow me." Jack grabs the container of whipped cream and adds it to the bottom of the mug. Then he pours in the coffee I just brewed, the premeasured spices I have sitting in a jar, a dollop of pumpkin puree, and then more whipped cream.

"You can't put that much whipped cream into a coffee!" I say, horrified.

"Oh yeah, watch me!" He has a gleam in his eye.

So I do. He keeps adding more and more whipped cream, and it towers precariously over the top of the coffee mug. He takes a sip, and he has whipped cream all over his mouth, nose, and somehow even his cheeks. He looks adorable, and again reminds me of a little kid, so innocent. I can't help it; I start laughing.

"What's so funny?" he asks, a dollop of whipped cream falling off his face and onto the counter with a loud splat.

And then I'm laughing harder, and he's laughing, too. The more whipped cream that falls off his face, the harder we both laugh. Then he takes a scoop of whipped cream off his face and sticks it on the tip of my nose. His touch is surprisingly gentle and takes my breath away. We both stop laughing.

"Maybe we're approaching this all wrong," he says, looking at me seriously.

"Oh yeah? How so?" I ask, my voice suddenly serious, too.

"Maybe we need to turn the pumpkin spice latte into a five-senses experience. You need to feel the pumpkin spice latte, to be the pumpkin spice latte, in order to truly enjoy one."

I start laughing again, harder this time, and he does, too.

"So we should turn it into some kind of . . . performance art?"

He snaps his fingers. "Bingo."

"A true multisensory experience," I say.

"Yes!" he practically shouts.

"So how do we do that?"

He shrugs. "I don't know. Any ideas?"

"No. You?"

We look at the whipped cream spilling from the mug.

"Well, pictures seem like a good place to start?" I take out my phone, snap some pictures of the overflowing mug. Then I look at Jack, still with whipped cream on his face, and get some pictures of him, too. He sticks out his tongue and crosses his eyes, and I snap more pictures.

"I'm not the only participant in this performance!" He looks at my phone in my hands. "May I?"

He takes my phone, snaps some pictures of me now, from all kinds of ridiculous angles, and I should *feel* ridiculous, whipped cream on my nose, putting myself in silly poses, making goofy faces. But I don't.

"What do you think?" Jack asks, flipping through my photos.

I start laughing again. "I think we're no closer to figuring out the perfect pumpkin spice latte."

"Right! Time to be serious!" He salutes me, but with whipped cream all over his face, the overall effect has me laughing again.

"What? Do I have something on my face?" Jack asks. "I feel like I have a little something right here." He wipes at his face, nowhere close to where the whipped cream is. "Did I get it?"

"No!" I say, doubled over in laughter.

"Now?" he asks, wiping even farther away from the whipped cream.

I shake my head, laughing too hard to speak.

"Well, you have a little something right here," he says, pointing to his nose.

I wipe my nose.

"Oh, and here, too," he says, swiping whipped cream on my cheek.

I'm surprised again by the gentleness of his touch.

Suddenly, neither of us is laughing.

We look at each other. I reach out and wipe the whipped cream off his cheek. "I think I got it."

"Good," he says quietly.

And then, we hear my front door opening, and we jump apart. I quickly wipe the whipped cream off my face with a kitchen towel, and I see Jack doing the same.

My mom comes in, carrying a bag of groceries. "What happened in here?" She's surveying the whipped cream—on the counter, on the floor, everywhere—and the pumpkin spice latte, which is also overflowing with whipped cream.

"Oh . . . just some . . . experimenting!" I say. Does my voice sound shrill?

"I'm so sorry we made a mess," Jack says, cleaning the whipped cream off the floor.

"It's fine," my mom says. But she just watches us, her arms crossed against her chest, a bemused look on her face.

"There!" Jack says, standing up. "I think I got it all! I should get going. It's almost dinnertime."

"Oh, right," I say, turning to look at my mom, who is finally unloading her grocery bag.

"Bye, Ms. Kane," Jack says.

My mom turns around again. "I hope you guys had some fun and didn't spend the whole time talking about pumpkin spice lattes?"

Jack's eyes meet mine. "I think we had a lot fun," he says. "Right, Lucy?"

I nod, smiling. "We did."

My mom smiles. "Good!" she says, then goes back to unpacking her groceries.

I walk Jack to the front door. "Thanks for the help."

He laughs. "Help?"

"Right. *Fun*. Thank you for the *fun*."

"It was my pleasure, Lucy."

We look at each other in silence again, until Jack nods. "Right. See you tomorrow?"

I nod back. "Yep! Tomorrow!" Okay, my voice is definitely still shrill.

Why has Jack made my voice shrill?

That night, when I'm taking a break from my homework, I thumb through my photos: the whipped cream on the floor, and spilling out of the mug; Jack's goofy faces; my own smiling face. I can't believe how happy I look while I'm trying to make a pumpkin spice latte.

I can't believe how happy I look around Jack Harper.

I post a picture of the whipped cream, and, at the last second, a picture of my own smiling face.

I close out the app and open my texts.

Amber

> Happy girl. What made you so happy?

Lucy

> Long story.

Amber

> I have time.

Lucy

> It's part of the Great Pumpkin Spice Latte Creation Project.

Amber

> Sounds like a short story?

Lucy

> I'll make it a longer story tomorrow at lunch?

Amber

Deal.

Lucy

Deal.

And then a text from Jack:

Jack

I think we've been approaching this pumpkin spice latte thing all wrong. Can we have another Great Pumpkin Spice Latte Creation Project meeting tomorrow?

Lucy

Sure.

Jack

Sure?

Lucy

Sure.

Jack

Sure!

Lucy

Should I be more enthusiastic?

Jack

Maybe?

Lucy

Maybe I'll be more enthusiastic after I hear this idea of yours.

Jack

Fair enough. I'll stop by after your Cup o' Jo shift?

Lucy

Roger that.

Jack

Roger.

23

When I'm sitting in homeroom the next day, trying to get myself organized, trying to remember when my algebra quiz is, a shadow falls across my desk. I look up, and Melanie is standing above me.

"Hi?" I say.

"Your Cup o' Jo stuff is cool," she says.

"Thanks?" I say uncertainly.

She looks like she wants to say more, so I wait while she gathers her thoughts. "It's cool what you and your mom do," she says finally. "Really cool."

I've been going to school with Melanie since kindergarten, and this may be the longest conversation I've ever had with her. Definitely the weirdest.

"Thanks," I say again, with I hope more certainty in my voice this time.

She stands at my desk just a second longer, then nods like something has been decided, and sits down in her seat.

I'm trying to create the perfect pumpkin spice latte. With Jack Harper. And now Melanie is talking to me. What alternate universe have I entered?

The rest of my morning passes with me in a strange haze, trying to process my new reality, and when it's finally time for lunch, I'm relieved for some solid, familiar ground with Evie and Amber. This I know. This I can do.

Except as soon as I sit down, Evie says, "Can we talk about the Great Pumpkin Spice Latte Creation Project?"

"Can we not?" I say, sighing.

"Can we talk about those pictures at least, please?" Amber pleads. She pulls out her phone, opens my most recent photos. "Hello, that smile!"

I feel another smile on my face as I look at the picture, and the previous day with Jack returns to my mind.

"There it is again!" Amber says.

"Are you blushing?" Evie asks, peering at my face.

"No!" I immediately say, feeling my cheeks get even redder.

Amber says, "Yeah, you definitely owe us an explanation or two."

"There isn't much to explain!" I say. "I think Jack and I were feeling a little . . . silly? Punchy? Too much sugar and pumpkin spice lattes. And too much whipped cream." I'm talking fast, and my friends give me confused looks.

"And this is the same Jack that you called a lying liar, right?" Evie asks.

I nod.

"Okay, just checking," she says.

"I know. It's weird. It's all so weird. But Cup o' Jo's social media stuff is getting bigger, and I want to get this pumpkin spice latte perfect and—"

"What about the new desserts you were making?" Evie interrupts.

"Huh?" I ask, trying to make the connection between pumpkin spice lattes and desserts.

"Those new desserts you made, remember? The cupcakes?" she says.

"Oh, right. One was a muffin," I say impatiently.

"Whatever," she says, waving her hand. "How have those been doing? Have you made any other new desserts or pastries?"

"No," I say. " I haven't really had time."

I see my friends exchange a look.

"What?" I snap.

"Just . . . are you maybe taking this pumpkin spice latte thing a little too seriously? A little too far? Putting a little too much pressure on yourself?" Evie asks.

"Are you kidding me? You were the one who told me to work

with Jack in the first place!" I glare at Amber accusingly. "And you were just saying how happy I look in my pictures. The ones where I'm trying to create the perfect pumpkin spice latte!"

"I know, I know," Amber says. "We've just been—"

"Everything is *fine*, guys, okay? I don't want to talk about it anymore!"

We eat the rest of our lunch in silence. So much for a normal lunch with my friends.

I'm so grateful when it's time for English class. Because it's the last class of my completely weird day. And also maybe a teeny bit because I'll see Jack. Not that I'm happy to see him or anything, but I'm wondering if maybe he'll give me some clues about what his new plan of attack is for the perfect pumpkin spice latte. But he slides into his desk just as Mrs. Ryan starts class, and I hate that I feel disappointed.

Toward the end of class, I look at the clock on the wall in the back of the room, and Jack winks at me. I'm still trying to figure out why he's winking at me when the bell rings and class is over. The school day is over. I'm in such a fog that by the time I get my stuff packed, Jack is already gone.

Which is probably for the best. I don't trust any interactions with anyone at school right now.

When I get to Cup o' Jo, Sheva, Danielle, and Will, a very part-time employee, are all behind the counter. "Hey, you!" Will says, smiling as I slip my apron on.

"Hey," I say back, slightly confused. We haven't had to call him in a while. We haven't been busy enough to need him.

"I think all your social media stuff is increasing business," Sheva says, reading my mind. "Your mom called Will around nine this morning. Been busy all day." She yawns, to prove her point.

My mom walks up from the back storeroom carrying napkins. She looks tired.

"Busy day I hear?" I say to my mom.

But she looks happy, too. "I think your posts are doing it, Lucy."

"You think?" I say skeptically. "But I haven't even made the perfect pumpkin spice latte yet!"

My mom laughs, but I say, "Mom, I'm serious. It's almost the weekend, it's almost Halloween, and I still can't make the perfect drink, and if you were busy today, the weekend is going to be even busier and—"

"Lucy," my mom interrupts. "It's okay. Customers are fine with the latte we have."

"But I don't want fine!" I say. "I want the best. I will make the best. And, actually, Jack told me he has some genius idea, so we're going to do some more pumpkin spice latte work after my shift."

My mom sighs. "Okay. But, honey, please tell me this is the last one of these pumpkin spice latte sessions."

"You mean Great Pumpkin Spice Latte Creation Project sessions."

"Yes, whatever you guys are calling it," my mom says impatiently. "Please tell me it's the last one?"

I cross my arms. "Why?"

She pauses, searching for the right words. "Because I'm worried about how much time you're spending on this."

"Oh, not you too."

"Not *me too* what?"

"Nothing," I say quickly.

She looks at me, her eyebrow raised.

I sigh. "Amber and Evie probably think I'm working on the drink too hard also, and why is everyone suddenly so concerned about me?"

"Lucy, please, don't drive yourself crazy over this drink, okay?"

I wave my hand. "Okay, okay."

A group of customers comes in and we all set to work. I don't get a chance to talk to my mom again until my shift is over.

"I'll see you soon," I tell her, and give her a quick hug. "I'm off to make the perfect pumpkin spice latte."

"Remember what I said! This is the last time!"

"We'll see!" I answer vaguely.

I don't look back as I leave the shop because I can't deal with anyone else worrying about me or even sharing a meaningful glance about me. I've had enough of that lately to last me a lifetime.

24

A few minutes after I get home, Jack rings my doorbell.

I let him in, and before he even says anything, he scoops up Pancakes. I can't believe how normal it feels to watch him pick up my cat. To have him in my house.

"So what is this revelation you've had?" I ask.

"I think we're trying to bring everything together too soon," he says.

"Huh?" I ask, confused. "Are you speaking metaphorically or literally?"

"Literally!" he says. "I think we're trying to, uh, unite the flavors before they're ready."

"Are you sure you're not speaking metaphorically?"

"Yes!" he says. "Just think about it."

"Yeah, still no clue."

"Okay, hear me out. I was looking up recipes on YouTube—"

"Are you serious?"

"Yes! I was thinking about other fall recipes. *Autumnal* recipes," he says, grinning. "Thought maybe I'd find inspiration or something. And then, I found a recipe for apple cider."

He looks at me, waiting for me to catch on, which I'm not.

"It simmers!" he finally says, exasperated. "For hours."

I hate to admit it, but what he's saying starts to make sense. "So should we simmer the pumpkin? That'll make it more flavorful? But won't it just completely dissolve the pumpkin?"

"Not if we add other things to it first. Sugar, spice—"

"And everything nice?" I joke.

He gives me a dirty look.

"Sorry, sorry," I say, thinking. But what he's saying starts to slowly sink in. "So, a syrup of sorts?"

"Exactly!"

"And then add the syrup to the coffee?" I say, still thinking out loud.

"I think you're getting it."

"Of *course* I'm getting it!" I say impatiently. "So make a syrup, but it needs to simmer first, bringing all the flavors together slowly. And the syrup should have—"

"Real pumpkin!" we both say at the same time.

"We were trying to unite too many flavors too quickly," I say, almost in a daze. "Well, let's slow things down!"

I look at Jack, and he seems to be feeling some of the excitement I am. "Yes! You're putting it into actual words better than I could."

"So any thoughts on what we should add to this syrup?" I ask him. "I mean, besides our fresh pumpkin puree?"

"Oh, I was figuring you'd know what to do about that part, like usual."

"Let me think about it," I say. I pull out my pumpkin spice mix, give it another appreciative sniff, then stick the jar in Jack's face. "Tell me what you smell."

He puts his hand over mine as he holds the jar. Our faces are very close, and I look into his sparkling green eyes. He looks back, and we stand there like that, until he finally gives a hesitant sniff. "Cloves for sure."

We both laugh, and he's so close I can feel his breath on my cheek. "Cinnamon? Ginger?" He keeps sniffing.

"Very good," I say quietly.

He pulls back abruptly, letting go of my hand, then sneezes.

We both laugh, though I miss the warmth of his hand already. "Nutmeg and allspice, too," I say.

"Got it."

We look at each other again, and I force myself to break eye contact with him, though it feels almost physically impossible.

"Let's get this started." I grab a saucepan and fill it with about a cup of water, then add a cup of sugar.

Jack is watching me, an excited look on his face.

I dissolve the sugar in simmering water, then I add in my premade spice mix.

Jack inhales deeply, and I find myself doing the same. My kitchen smells amazing.

"Don't bring things together before they're ready," I mutter.

I pull out the jar of homemade pumpkin puree. "How much are you going to put in?" he asks.

I look at him, the son of Java Junction owners, standing here in my kitchen, helping me craft a pumpkin spice latte. The surrealness of the moment does not escape me.

"Less is more? Or more is less?" he says.

"Not sure." I add two tablespoons of the puree, but the mix still seems too liquid. I add another tablespoon, but still too liquid. "What do you think? A smidge more?"

He grins. "A big smidge."

I add a final tablespoon of pumpkin, and finally—*finally!*—the texture seems right.

"Now we wait," I say.

"How long?" Jack asks eagerly.

I shrug and set the kitchen timer. "Let's start with fifteen minutes?"

"Longest fifteen minutes ever," he says, and I laugh.

He looks around my kitchen, then squints his eyes at my fridge.

"What?" I ask, following his eyes.

"Is that you?" He's pointing to a picture my mom hung up on the fridge with a magnet. It's me, when I was in kindergarten, in the witch costume my mom made for me for Halloween.

"No, it's my sister," I deadpan.

Jack says defensively, "Look how light your hair is in the picture! When did it get so much darker?"

"It's not that much darker," I say, protectively grabbing at my messy bun.

He looks at me, a little smile on his lips, and before he can say anything else, I say, "That was one of my favorite Halloweens. And not just because my mom made an awesome costume."

"Whoa, your mom made you your costume?" he says. "Like, you didn't just go to Target and pick one out?"

I laugh. "She did that year. I can't remember why. Maybe guilt about how much she was working? Cup o' Jo was still in its early days then, and she was working a lot. Anyway. I remember the costume and trick-or-treating with her and Amber and Amber's moms. I think Amber was a Power Ranger that year."

"And?" Jack looks at me expectantly.

"And what?"

"What made that Halloween so special for you, do you think? What makes it one of your favorites?"

I pause, considering the question. "You know, I don't even know for sure what it is. I just remember everything felt so perfect that night. I didn't want it to end. Sorry, I guess that's kind of boring." I shrug.

"Favorites don't always have to have some complicated reason why they're our favorites. Sometimes it's just as simple as everything felt perfect. Everything felt right."

"Yeah, that's exactly it!" I say. "Everything did feel so right." I think about being five again, remembering the feel of the witch costume sleeves on my arms.

Jack smiles.

"Well, what about you?" I ask. "What was your favorite Halloween?"

"It was when I was in fourth grade. We were in Chicago. It actually snowed that year." He laughs, remembering. "But we lived in a big apartment building, so it didn't really matter. We went trick-or-treating up and down the hallways. A lot of people had their doors open, just hanging out, and kids were running into different apartments, playing together. And it felt like I belonged somewhere, I think? Like this community you have in Briar Glen. I think I felt it that Halloween." He looks at me. "It's silly, right?"

I realize we've moved closer to each other.

I'm looking at his long eyelashes as I say, "I love that. Everything felt perfect. Everything felt right."

"Yeah," he says in an equally quiet voice.

The timer goes off, making both of us jump.

"Do you think it's been enough time?" I ask.

Jack shrugs.

"Well, here goes nothing." I strain the liquid, then pour it into a jar, and wow, it smells amazing. I quickly brew the espresso and add it to a mug, then add maple syrup and vanilla. I froth the milk, then look at the pumpkin syrup. "We're thinking more is less, right?"

Jack shrugs again.

I take a deep breath and pour what seems like a good amount of the syrup mixture into the coffee, then add the frothed milk, whipped cream, and cinnamon.

I hold the steaming mug between Jack and me. "You get first sip," he says. "You did all the work."

"Yeah, but it was your idea!" I say. "But also, this smells too amazing." I take a sip. A little sip. I close my eyes, savoring the taste.

Then I go to the spice cabinet and pull out crushed cloves.

Jack laughs. "Please tell me you're joking with those evil things," he says.

"A smidge," I say, picking up a tiny amount between my

fingers and sprinkling it into the drink.

"I thought a smidge could never be used as a unit of measurement," Jack says.

I barely hear him because I'm too busy drinking the pumpkin spice latte.

And suddenly, I feel it in my bones, and it sounds cheesy, but I feel it in my heart. It's like when I'm baking and after so many test runs—tinkering and adjusting and adapting—I've finally created the perfect recipe.

"Try it!" I say, handing him the drink. I watch him eagerly, and when I see his face, I know it. We did it.

"Jack Harper, I think we've done it! I think we've finally created the perfect pumpkin spice latte!" Before I know what I'm doing, I'm grabbing the drink out of his hands, putting it down, and throwing my arms around him in a huge hug.

I feel his arms wrapping around my waist.

He smells like the perfect latte we just made, and like something else really good, too—his hair gel or his shampoo, maybe? Or maybe it's just . . . *him*?

But wait, why am I hugging Jack Harper?

I pull away, take a step back, feeling my cheeks flush with embarrassment. "Sorry," I say quickly. "I think I got carried away in the excitement of the moment."

Jack clears his throat, scratches the back of his neck, and says in a low voice, "Don't worry about it."

There is a gravelly edge to his voice I've never noticed before.

"So now what?" I say. "Well, first of all, do you agree? Is this the drink? Like, this is the drink, right?" I realize I'm talking really fast, but I'm not totally sure why.

"I think you know it is," he says, his voice sounding kind of weird, too.

"So now what?" I ask again.

"So now you get that drink on Cup o' Jo's menu stat and sell the heck out of it."

"You make it sound so easy! You make everything sound so easy!"

He shrugs. "It'll be easy because it's a good drink. Because you made a good drink."

"Do you ever get upset?"

"Upset?" he repeats, looking surprised.

"Yeah, you know, discontented. Frustrated. Just, your calmness, your confidence is—"

"Annoying?" he fills in.

"No." I think, searching for the right word. "Inspiring?"

"Thank you. That's nice." His cheeks redden. He suddenly seems the opposite of calm. "I do get upset, though. Sometimes. I also just happen to be incredibly forgiving. Like I said before, I don't want to just observe my life. I want to live it. And if that means I get my feelings hurt a few times, it's okay."

"Your feelings get hurt?" I can't keep the surprise out of my voice. I have a horrible thought. "Have I ever . . ." I trail off because, looking at his face, I know that I have hurt his feelings. "I'm sorry."

"What are you sorry for?"

"If I ever hurt your feelings," I say quietly, my head down, not able to look at him.

He doesn't say anything, and I finally sneak a peek at him. He's not looking at me—I think he's looking out the kitchen window—but there's an expression on his face I've never seen before. His green eyes look different, and I realize it's because they don't have their usual sparkle. He turns his face back to me. "It's okay," he says, his voice quiet now, too. He clears his throat. "I mean, what do you think you need to be sorry for?" He's trying to smile, I think, but his eyes still seem sad.

"I'm so sorry for all the times I didn't trust you, or your intentions," I say. I know I'm just scratching the surface of things I want to apologize to him for.

"I knew you'd come around eventually," he says, his usual ease returning as quickly as it left, his eyes starting to sparkle again.

"You're way, way too forgiving," I say.

"Back to this drink!" he says, waving his hand.

"Right, the drink," I say, my head still spinning. "Are your parents going to be upset that you helped me?"

"I think they're happy that I'm finally showing an interest in something related to coffee," he says. "But stop worrying about it! Get this posted online and be ready to start selling a lot of pumpkin spice lattes."

"You make it sound like this will be an overnight success."

"People like their pumpkin spice lattes in these parts this time of year," he says.

I laugh, get out my phone, and start taking pictures of the drink.

I'm concentrating so hard that I don't notice that Jack has grabbed his jacket and is about to head out.

"Oh, you're leaving?" I say, unable to keep the disappointment out of my voice.

"I don't want to be a distraction," he says. "Now get to it!"

"Okay, okay," I say. "But wait!"

He comes back in the room, looking confused.

There are so many things I want to say, but I'm having trouble finding the right words. "Just . . . thank you. Again. For everything. And . . . I'm sorry. Again."

"It was nothing, kid," he says.

The door closes behind him, and I'm left standing, holding the pumpkin spice latte. I look at the drink in my hand. I think about all the work that went into it, all the different changes and adjustments I made to it along the way, starting with my first attempt, with the floating globs of pumpkin puree; to Jack's clove-heavy liquid potpourri version; the whipped cream on Jack's face, how adorable he was with it all over his face, the way he gently put whipped cream on my cheek. I realize I'm smiling—while holding a pumpkin spice latte while thinking about Jack Harper. My friends are telling me to stop working so hard, and my mom is, too, and Cup o' Jo is getting more and more popular on social media. Should I look out my window for flying pigs?

I try to focus on the drink, but it feels like I'm watching some-one else as I take a few quick pictures of the pumpkin spice latte, trying to capture the right lighting. Then I position myself in front of my mom's falling leaf dish towel. I snap a few more pic-tures of the coffee from different angles on the counter, and then I thumb through the results. I find the best picture, and then in the weird alternate universe I now live in, I post the image, along with the caption: *New #pumpkinspicelatte starting tomorrow morning!* to Cup o' Jo's social media account.

I text my mom.

Lucy

New and improved pumpkin spice latte. DONE.

Mom

I saw! Looks so good. And very happy you're DONE. Proud of you, honey. We'll start selling it tomorrow? It is a Saturday.

Lucy

That's the plan, right?

Mom

That's the plan.

I start a text to Amber and Evie, then remember I'm mad at them. Besides, they'll see Cup o' Jo's post, know that I've finally crafted the perfect pumpkin spice latte. I put my phone down in the kitchen and head upstairs to take a shower.

About an hour later, I hear my mom come home. She's in the kitchen, pulling takeout containers out of a bag when I get downstairs.

"Might want to check that post," she says, smiling.

"Why?" I ask slowly.

I pick up my phone as I open a container of tofu pad thai and nearly drop it again. There are a lot of likes. There are a lot of comments.

Can't wait to check out @CupoJo's psl!

Look how cute the shop is! The whole town! It's fall!

Quintessential fall!

Road trip!

Let's go this weekend.

I read through more and more comments, but then my mom grabs my phone out of my hands. "Okay, enough with the phone," she says. "Enough with the pumpkin spice latte already! People on the internet can say anything, right?"

"They can, and they do, but maybe you'll need to call Will again this weekend."

My mom chuckles as she scoops chicken massaman curry onto her plate. "I might. But seriously, enough with the drink talk!"

I take my plate to our table but don't start eating yet. "I thought you were proud of me? Excited for the new drink?" I realize I might be whining a bit.

"I *am* proud of you!" she says as she sits down next to me. "So proud of you. But I don't like how much of your attention this drink has taken."

I don't feel like having a repeat of the conversation I've already

254

had with her, and with my friends, so I just eat my tofu pad thai without another mention of pumpkin spice lattes.

After dinner, I grab my phone from the counter, and it's filled with notifications. More likes and comments on the pumpkin spice latte post, and a text.

Jack

Nice work, kid.

I smile, start to write him back, but then look through the rest of my texts, looking for something, anything from my friends. Nothing. Absolutely nothing.

I text Jack instead.

Lucy

Couldn't have done it without you!

Jack

It was my autumnal delight.

I smile, wanting to say more, but suddenly I'm starting to feel tired of my phone. And besides, it might be a busy day at Cup o' Jo tomorrow and I need to rest.

Maybe.

25

When I wake up the next morning, my first thought is of pumpkin spice lattes. Today is the day. I hop out of bed and am dressed and ready to go before my mom is even awake. I'm sitting on the couch, reading through more comments on my newest post when my mom comes downstairs.

"How long have you been awake?" she asks, yawning.

I shrug. "I don't know. A while. Are you almost ready?"

She laughs as she puts on her boots. "Honey, we're just going to treat today like a normal day."

"Normal," I say. "Because it's so normal for me to make pumpkin spice lattes and post about them on social media and have people talk about coming to Cup o' Jo just for the drink. Right. Totally normal." There is a weird high pitch to my voice, which I realize is excitement.

"Let's not get too excited about anything just yet, okay?"

"Who's excited?" I say, opening the front door.

She yawns again, and we start our walk to the shop, my mom her usual sleepy self, while I feel myself thrumming with excitement and anticipation.

As we round the corner to Cup o' Jo, we see a group of people on the sidewalk outside the shop, some of them peering into the windows.

My mom quickens her pace, and I do, too.

As we get closer, the people seem happy to see us.

"May I help you?" my mom asks the crowd.

"Oh, sorry we're so early," one of the women says. "We're a bunch of early risers, and we wanted to try this new pumpkin spice latte."

"New pumpkin spice latte," my mom echoes. "Of course! Let us just get everything set up for the day and we'll welcome you in."

"No problem!" the woman says.

My mom looks at me, slightly dazed, and I think I look slightly dazed, too, but I follow her into the shop.

Sheva, Danielle, and Will all arrive soon after, looking just as dazed.

I show them how to make a huge batch of pumpkin syrup, then a pumpkin spice latte.

"Is it time to get excited yet?" I ask my mom a few minutes before seven.

"Maybe a little."

She unlocks the door, says, "Ready?"

"Ready."

Then we start our busiest day at Cup o' Jo since Java Junction moved in.

Sometime mid-morning while I'm making yet another pumpkin spice latte, I look around at the sea of customer faces in line, milling around the shop, and sitting at our tables and realize I don't recognize a lot of people. I should be thrilled to see our shop so busy. Ecstatic that I finally created the perfect drink. And I am excited thinking about how good this will be for business, how it'll take away some of my mom's worries and bring financial stability to the shop. But still, it's strange to see my familiar shop, my second home, full of so many faces I don't recognize.

Then I see Mrs. Vervone's surprised face as she peers around the shop. When she gets to the front of the line, she says, "Wow! I've never seen you guys this busy!"

"It's weird, right?" I say, trying to smile, to show some excitement.

She laughs. "Just don't forget us little people, us locals."

"What? Never! We love our Briar Glen locals, our regulars!" I say.

She pats my hand encouragingly. "Honey, I'm kidding. You guys deserve all the success in the world."

I make her maple latte, my mind spinning in a million directions at once. I hand her the drink, and she quickly says, "You and your mom keep up the good work, okay?"

I nod, then help the next person, Molly Russell, another one of my former teachers. The rest of the morning is a blur. It ends up being not just our busiest Saturday since Java Junction opened, but also our busiest Saturday ever. I couldn't even guess how many pumpkin spice lattes we sell. A hundred? A million?

When my mom closes the door, she just says, "Well!"

"Normal day, right?" I say, slumping down in one of the chairs.

"Totally," my mom says, joining me at the table.

Sheva emerges from the bathroom, cleaning supplies in hand, looking just as tired as I feel. Danielle is cleaning our coffee machine, and Will is tidying up the tables, picking up empty cups.

I pull my phone out of my pocket. It's been so busy all day I haven't had a chance to even look at it. Another flood of notifications fills my screen. Cup o' Jo has been tagged in a ton of posts. There is photo after photo of people holding pumpkin spice lattes. *My* pumpkin spice latte. With captions like *best #psl ever* and *Had this pumpkin spice latte in the cutest town!* and *Get to*

Briar Glen and get to Cup o' Jo for a psl. The posts go on and on.

I also have a ton of texts from my friends:

Amber

I'm sorry.

Evie

Hey that was weird yesterday. I'm sorry. Your new pumpkin spice latte looks awesome.

Then, later in the day:

Amber

Holy cow! Lucy, you're famous!

Evie

Well, your drink is famous.

I have more texts, too, from other friends and family members, but I can barely read them I'm so overwhelmed.

I keep scrolling through notifications and texts, and see one from Jack: *Told you it was a good drink.*

I look up and see my mom looking at me. "What?" I ask.

"Sorry, just processing the day."

I put my phone down. "Yeah, me too."

We're both quiet for a second.

"So I think today was good for busine—"

"Lucy," my mom interrupts.

"Sorry, no more talk about money, got it."

I pick up my phone to write back to my friends, write back to Jack, and post something on Cup o' Jo's social media, but I realize I don't know what to say.

26

I'm actually happy to go to school on Monday, which is weird. As much as I don't want to admit it, I am feeling a little burnt out from the weekend.

I pull my books from my locker, thinking how odd it is that I wanted Cup o' Jo to be busy, and now we are, but things feel strange. I'm deep in thought when Gus Rivera stops by. He's another person I've known since kindergarten but have probably only talked to twice in my life. Well, I guess it's about to be a third.

I open my mouth to speak, but he's already talking. "You and your mom are turning Briar Glen into a tourist trap," he says, glaring at me.

"Happy Monday to you, too," I say.

He doesn't crack a smile.

"I'm sorry?" I say. Though am I sorry? And what am I even sorry for? "It's always like this in the fall. I think people forget every year how many leaf peepers we get—"

"Yeah, well, your leaf peepers were blocking my driveway. I was late for school!"

"Wait, why is this my fault?" I ask. "What does Cup o' Jo have to do with any of this?"

"Because I looked in their car, and I saw Cup o' Jo coffee cups!"

"Look, I'm sorry you were late, but the coffee shop is my mom's business. It's how we pay our bills, how she buys our food," I say, feeling protective of my mom, and her shop.

He snorts. "Well, can you remind your customers how to park, please? Or, I dunno, put in a parking lot like Java Junction?"

At the mention of Java Junction, I think of Jack, but I also think of how his parents' business is why I got into this mess in the first place.

"Put up some signs at your house about not blocking the drive-way; I don't know!" I snap, slamming my locker shut. "Thanks for supporting local businesses, really." I walk away before he can say anything else.

I don't have any other conversations like that, but I swear people are looking at me funny the rest of the morning. By the time I get to lunch, I'm so happy to see my friends, I hug them.

"Well, if it isn't the mayor of Briar Glen!" Evie says.

"What?" I ask.

Evie says, "Whoa, dude, was just a joke."

"Sorry. Just . . . everything is weird."

Amber says, "I'm sure it'll die down soon. You guys just unveiled the new drink this weekend."

"But we don't want things to die down!" I point out. "We need the business."

"You're still getting used to this," Amber says.

"Used to what?"

"Used to Cup o' Jo blowing up on social media," Amber says.

"I don't know if blowing up is the right way to describe it," I say. But even as the words leave my mouth, I'm not entirely sure they're true. I've been too tired to spend much time on Cup o' Jo's socials.

Evie snickers and pulls out her phone. "I think ten thousand followers counts as blowing up."

I almost choke on my sandwich. "Last I checked we had a few thousand followers."

"And when was that? When dinosaurs roamed the earth?" Evie jokes. "Keep up with the times!"

I look at Amber and Evie, suddenly feeling panic-stricken and confused. "But this is good, right?"

My friends echo their assent, and I hope they're right. But I'm not so sure that they are.

My eyes wander to Jack's table. He waves at me, and I wave back. His eyes are all sparkly, and he and his silly sparkly eyes definitely don't hurt things at all.

When I get to English class, I stop by Jack's desk. "Thanks again for the advice on the drink."

He laughs. "I'd say it was a success?"

"Yeah." I want to say more; there are so many things in my head. But I don't even know where to begin, and just then Mrs. Ryan walks into the room.

When class is over, I try to catch Jack's eye again, but he's talking to one of his soccer dudes, so I just give him a little wave.

Usually Mondays at Cup o' Jo are pretty quiet, but when I arrive, the shop is packed. I slip my apron on. "Another busy day?"

"Our busiest Monday in years!" my mom responds, looking happy but tired, too.

"Some of this craziness will die down, right?"

"I'm sure," she says. "You know how things on social media go."

"Do you still think it was a good idea for me to make a new pumpkin spice latte?"

"Did making the new drink make *you* happy?"

I think again about Jack and all the time I spent with him, and I smile. "Yeah, it did."

"Good," she says. "That's all that really matters."

Then I get to work, serving up pumpkin spice lattes until closing time.

27

The next morning, I wake up before my alarm. I had strange dreams all night, and I don't feel rested at all, but I pick up my phone, anyway. It's filled with notifications about Cup o' Jo, and I also see a string of texts from my friends telling me to check my Instagram. I figure they're probably just talking about some celebrity I don't care about, but whatever, I'll bite. I open Cup o' Jo's account, and *oh*. I see what they're talking about.

Uh, I just had the best #pumpkinspicelatte. At @CupoJo in some New England town called Briar Glen.

Oh come on, nothing can beat @JavaJunction's pumpkin spice latte.

Cup o' Jo totally revamped their PSL. Did you know for a while they didn't even serve them?

Where is Briar Glen anyway?

My family and I went to Briar Glen this weekend, and Cup o' Jo's PSL blows Java Junction's PSL out of the water.

And then:

Um, hello, #psl challenge between Java Junction and Cup o' Jo. It needs to happen. Everyone who agrees, comment!

Below this post, comment after comment of people saying **yes, 100 percent, such a good idea.**

And then more comments from people wondering who should do the challenge, people tagging their friends—I even see some names I recognize!—saying they want to do the challenge. I almost stop scrolling, but then I see it:

Trissylovesfall: **You can count me in! @JavaJunctionBriarGlen, @CupoJo check your DMs!**

With shaking hands, I open my messages, and toward the top is a message from Trissy—the influencer with nearly one million followers.

Hey @CupoJo, I'm totally up for this challenge! The sooner the better? How about this weekend? It's so close to Halloween!

I write back with shaking hands: *Sounds good!*

Trissy is online, active, and I see her writing a reply. *What's your phone number? Will give you a call this afternoon? I'm talking to Java Junction then, too.*

I give her my phone number, wondering if maybe this is all some kind of dream? I get out of bed, stretch a few times. Nope. I'm definitely awake. While I've been online, I've felt my phone buzzing with texts. My friends are texting, asking what is going on, and then my phone rings. It's my mom. Oh my gosh, my mom! She's at work right now; does she even know what's happening?

"Mom!" I say. "You won't believe—"

"I just saw!" she says. "We're going to have an influencer? Did you get in touch with her yet? When is she coming?"

"This weekend, I guess? Really soon!"

"Wow! This is amazing!"

My phone keeps buzzing, and then I realize my alarm is going off, and my mom quickly says, "Get to school! We'll talk about it this afternoon."

"School! Yes! I need to go to school."

"Yes, you do!" she says, laughing.

"Okay, I love you! I can't believe this is happening!"

"I love you, too, honey! I can't, either! Talk soon," she says, and hangs up.

I look at my phone in my hand, still buzzing with texts and

notifications. Including messages from Jack. But I don't have time to read anything from him. I really don't have time to keep reading comments, either, because it really is getting late. An influencer. At Cup o' Jo. Deciding if our pumpkin spice latte is better than Java Junction's. Because of our pumpkin spice latte.

A pumpkin spice latte I made.

I get to my desk in homeroom just as the last bell is ringing, phone still in my hand. I'd been texting my friends on my walk to school, filling them in on the latest, and there were more texts from Jack, asking if we could talk at lunch. I write *okay*, then turn my phone off.

I slide my phone into my bag and look up to find a bunch of people staring at me, including Margaret McAlister, who sits to my right. She's never been a close friend of mine or anything, but she's also lived in Briar Glen all her life. I meet her eyes, but she looks away quickly and then stares at her textbook on her desk.

Nick Robertson, who sits in front of me, turns around and whispers, "Dude! Trissy is coming to Briar Glen! How did you swing that?!"

I shrug. "I didn't swing anything!"

He laughs. "You are too cool."

"Thanks? I think?"

He laughs again. "I hear that she has pumpkin pie spice in her body instead of blood."

I giggle, which makes Mrs. Perry look up from her desk. "This is quiet time," she chides.

"Sorry," I say, feeling my face flush.

Margaret is looking at me again, but just like before, when I catch her eye, she goes back to staring at her textbook.

Finally, the bell signifying the end of homeroom rings, and Margaret looks at me again and finally speaks. "You know that this doesn't make you famous or anything, right?"

"I'm sorry?" I say.

"Just because you got some influencer to come here. You're not famous now."

"I never said I was," I say, confused.

"Don't let this go to your head. And especially don't turn Briar Glen into some kind of influencer haven."

She walks away before I have a chance to reply, so I just stand there, feeling the most confused and conflicted I've ever felt in my life.

Word quickly gets out about Trissy, and throughout the morning my classmates tell me how they think Trissy coming to Briar Glen is either super cool or definitely not. And my mind still spins, trying to process it all.

By the time I finally make it to the cafeteria, I'm exhausted. Even trying to get to my seat, it seems everyone has something to say to me.

I eventually make it to my table, but just as I'm about to sit, Jack frantically waves at me. I want nothing more than to talk to my friends, to digest the insanity of my morning, of what is happening, but I know I need to talk to him.

I walk to his table, feeling all eyes of the cafeteria on the two of us, but I'm past the point of caring. I have so many questions for him.

"Um," we both say at the same time as I sit down.

"This is crazy, right?" he whispers.

"Should we even be talking? Aren't you technically my competition now?"

"Seriously?" he asks.

"I don't know!" I look around the cafeteria, and people are just openly staring at us. I think someone even has their phone out, taking video, but I ignore it. Ignore everything. "What did you want to talk to me about so badly, anyway?"

"I don't know," he says. "Just how bananas this all is. I wanted to process it with you."

"Maybe we should process this all after we both talk to Trissy?" I finally say.

"Yeah. Good call. I think your friends might kill me if I keep you here any longer."

I look at my table, Evie and Amber staring at me expectantly. "Ha, yeah, I see what you mean. I'll talk to you later, I guess?"

"Yeah." He nods. "Maybe I can walk you to work after school and we can talk more?"

"I'd like that," I say. We both give each other another quick look, and I finally make it to my friends.

"What took you so long?" Evie asks.

"I don't even know where to begin," Amber says. "Briar Glen's first influencer visit!"

Evie says, "So when is Trissy com—"

"GUYS!" I say, and they both look at me. "Sorry, I don't actually even know what I was going to say. I just can't believe any of this. People have been so weird with me all day, either acting like I'm some kind of snob, or they think it's cool that Trissy is coming, and I can't believe any of this!" I stop, realizing I need to breathe.

Evie shrugs. "People are just jealous."

"Jealous of what?" I say.

"Oh, c'mon, you have an *influencer* coming to your place," Amber says. "We don't want people thinking bad things about Cup o' Jo. You guys aren't some chain. Like someone else." She gives a quiet nod over to Jack.

"Chains aren't always bad," I say.

Amber looks appalled. "Are you serious? I can't keep up with you. One minute you're friends with him and the next you're convinced he's evil!"

"Well, it's even more confusing now that we're in this weird competition together!"

"The challenge has been put into play," Evie says in a deep voice.

"What?" Amber and I say at the same time.

She sighs. "I don't know! It was supposed to be my ominous reality TV narrator voice."

"Ominous!" I say, alarmed.

"I was just trying to help!" Evie says.

I glare at her. "Not helping!"

"So when is this all supposed to go down?" Amber asks.

"I guess we're talking tonight. But maybe this weekend?"

"This weekend!" they both say at once, which catches the attention of a few nearby tables. They start whispering and looking at Jack and me.

"How is this my life, guys?" I ask, running my hands through my hair.

"Well, it's certainly one way to drum up business," Evie says. "That's a positive, right?"

Amber says, "What are you going to wear?"

"Wear?" I ask, confused. "When?"

"When Trissy is here?" Amber says. "I'm sure you're going to be in some of her clips."

"Clips?" I repeat.

"Yeah, when Trissy is here, live streaming, she'll probably include you and your mom," Amber says.

"Clips?" I say again.

"Never mind," Amber says. "We can figure that out later."

"Clips?" I echo one more time, weakly.

"Dude, wear whatever, who cares!" Evie says.

"Right, who cares what I'll be wearing in front of thousands of people." I roll my eyes. "You know, this all just proves how much trouble pumpkin spice lattes cause! This is why I never trusted the darn drink to begin with!"

"Technically you won't be in front of thousands of people. Not like you're standing in some kind of arena or something," Evie says.

"Yeah, just the arena of the internet," I say.

She shrugs. "Just trying to help!"

"You know, where some people see trouble, others see opportunity," Amber says.

"You sound like Yoda," I say. My voice is muffled, though, because my head is in my hands.

"It's gonna be great!" Amber says, patting my hand.

I look up at her.

"Seriously, no matter what happens, whatever the outcome, it's pretty cool that Trissy is coming here because of your pumpkin spice latte. Can you at least admit that?" Amber says.

"Fine," I say, knowing she's right.

But I still put my head back down in my hands for the rest of lunch.

I wish I could keep my head down for the rest of the day, but I've got two more classes to get through after lunch. By the time I make it to English class, I think I've talked to almost every single person at my high school.

"So, Pieface," Jayden asks as I sit down. "Can you put in a good word for me with Trissy?" He wags his eyebrows at me.

"Don't be a creeper," Jeff says, elbowing Jayden in the ribs.

Other people are trying to talk to me, but their faces are all starting to blend together. I look back at Jack, and he has a similar group of people around him.

"Help," we both mouth to each other at the same time.

Mrs. Ryan is at the front of the classroom, ignoring the chaos, until finally she yells, "Enough!"

That gets everyone's attention, and for the next forty minutes I get to think about a Dickensian world that doesn't include pumpkin spice lattes or influencers.

When class is over, I pack up quickly and meet Jack outside. He looks just as dazed as I feel. We walk in silence for a few minutes until I finally say, "Well, that was certainly one of the strangest days of my life!"

Jack laughs. "Yeah, same."

"You're talking to Trissy tonight, too?"

"Yeah, at six."

"Cool, my mom and I are talking to her at five thirty."

We walk in silence a little longer, both of us still thinking.

"How do your parents feel about this?" I ask.

He shrugs. "They were mostly concerned about the legality of it all, since Java Junction is a franchise, but I guess Trissy's lawyer will talk to some lawyer at Java Junction?"

"Oh, I didn't think about that," I say. "The legal stuff."

"Well, I'm sure your mom did. And if not, it sounds like Trissy's got herself some hotshot attorney, so . . ."

"Right," I say. But something else is bugging me, too. "This won't make things . . . weird between Java Junction and Cup o' Jo, right?"

"What? A social media influencer coming to Briar Glen and declaring—live, online—who has the better pumpkin spice latte?" He must register the look of horror on my face, because he quickly adds, "That was supposed to be a joke."

"Right, a joke." I don't feel like pointing out to him that behind every joke is a little bit of truth.

The way he looks at me, I feel like he might be thinking the same thing, but neither of us gives the words actual volume. We turn onto Main Street, both of us still lost in thought.

"What are your plans for Halloween?" Jack asks after we've been quiet for a few blocks.

"I'm not sure," I say. "I usually help my mom hand out candy at the shop."

"Cool."

"But this year I think I want to go out with my friends, too." I don't even realize it's true until the words leave my mouth.

"Yeah?" Jack says.

I nod. "Yeah."

"Well, then, you should!" Jack says.

"You're right," I say as we reach our respective coffee shops. "Good luck on your call. Is that what I should say?"

He shrugs. "Beats me?"

I laugh and watch him walk into Java Junction. As the door closes behind him, I realize I didn't ask him about his own Halloween plans.

I walk into Cup o' Jo, and at first I don't know where I am, because there's a huge line of customers. I quickly wash my hands, then put on my apron and join my mom and Sheva at the counter.

"It's been like this all day!" my mom says. She looks even more tired than the day before, but still happy.

I quickly get to work. Kim Downing is my first customer. She's a senior at my high school, but she lives a few streets over from me, and we used to play together when I was little. I usually see her a lot during finals.

"Hey, Lucy," she says, smiling warmly.

"Pumpkin spice latte?" I ask.

"How did you know?" She laughs. "It's cool to see your shop doing so well," she says while I make her drink.

"Thanks, though the influencer thing feels really weird," I admit.

"I bet!" she says. "Just think, we live in such a beautiful place that an influencer wants to come here." She lowers her voice and looks around. "I hope you guys win the contest, too, by the way."

"Thank you," I say as I hand her the drink and she taps her credit card.

A few customers later, Jayden comes in. I've never seen him in Cup o' Jo before, or even anywhere near the shop.

"I know, it's weird I'm here. But I hope you guys win the contest. And not just because Trissy is totally hot."

"Thanks?" I say.

He looks at the menu. "I have no idea what I'm even supposed to order," he mutters.

"I hear the pumpkin spice latte is pretty good."

"Blech, I actually hate pumpkin-flavored anything," he says. "I know, also weird."

"Not that weird." I look around to make sure no one is listening. "I used to hate pumpkin spice lattes, too. Making them, drinking them, everything about them."

He looks at me in surprise. "Should you even be saying that out loud?"

"I've made peace with the drink," I say. "I realized I was making the wrong kind all along. That I had to wait to bring the flavors together."

Now he's giving me a blank stare. "Are we still talking about pumpkin spice lattes?"

I take a quick look across the street, where I can see Jack at work at Java Junction. "I'm not sure, actually."

"Okay, Pieface, I'll just have one of these cookie things," he says, pointing to our dessert case.

"It's a scone."

"Yeah, that," he says, as I hand it to him. "Uh, and good luck," he says quickly before he pays and leaves.

That might have been one of the most pleasant conversations I've ever had with Jayden.

Finally, it's five o'clock and we can close up the shop. After Sheva, Danielle, and Will leave, my mom asks, "So how was school today?"

I start laughing. "Probably one of the weirdest days of my life!"

"Oh, why is that?"

"Just that whole, you know, influencer coming to Briar Glen and to Cup o' Jo and deciding if our pumpkin spice latte is better than Java Junction's thing."

"Oh, that little thing," my mom says, waving her hand. Then she turns to look at me, and I see the exhaustion mixed with excitement on her face. "Is this really happening?"

I reread Trissy's message for the millionth time, and then slide my phone over to my mom.

She nods, reading. "Okay, yeah, this sounds pretty real."

"Really real," I say.

We both look at each other in stunned silence and then get back to cleaning.

Then, I start to doubt the whole thing. "Do you think we can trust Trissy?" I ask. "What if it's all some kind of prank? And Java Junction. What if this is some publicity stunt they decided to pull?" The idea has just occurred to me, but it's rapidly gaining momentum in my mind.

My mom laughs. "I talked to them this morning. They told me they had nothing to do with this, and I told them the same. I think there would be legal ramifications if it was all a stunt."

"Legal ramifications," I echo. I think for a second. "I can't believe I'm saying this. But I trust them. I trust Jack, too. Which feels silly."

"Lucy, trusting someone isn't silly," she says. "Did I mess up that lesson in parenting?" she says, rubbing her head.

"No, Mom, I actually think you got that part perfectly right."

"Thanks, honey," she says, smiling at me.

At five thirty, my mom and I are sitting at one of our tables. I'm holding my phone in my sweaty hands. At 5:31, my phone rings with a video call from an unknown number. My mom and I look at each other.

"Well, here goes nothing," I say, before I swipe to answer the call. A girl about my age is on the other end, and it takes my brain a second to realize that this isn't Trissy. "Um, hello?" I say, confused. A wrong phone number, so close to when Trissy and I agreed to talk?

The girl smiles back, though, quickly understanding my confusion, and says, "Hi, I'm Jaclyn, Trissy's assistant." Right.

Of course she has an assistant. "Trissy is totally bummed she couldn't make this chat, but she's at an event right now. She's so looking forward to meeting you this weekend, though!"

I know my mom feels just as out of her element as me, but as always she's able to quickly whip out her customer-service smile. "We're looking forward to it as well! And we're honored that she's coming to Briar Glen, and to Cup o' Jo. It's our very first influencer visit!"

Jaclyn smiles back, but she's looking at something else on her screen. "Right, so it's pretty standard paperwork I'm going to send over to Cup o' Jo's email address. We won't sue you and you won't sue us; what we record is our intellectual property, all that kinda stuff. It's the same paperwork we're sending to Java Junction. My mom runs a law firm here in the city, so I assure you this is all airtight, standard stuff."

"Great! We'll keep an eye out for it," my mom says.

Jaclyn is looking back at us again, and says, "Any questions?"

I know I should speak, or do something. I look at my mom in a panic. Why am I so nervous?

"I can't think of any. Do you have any, Lucy?" my mom asks, looking at me meaningfully.

"Nothing right now. But, um, yeah, we're excited to meet you! I mean, Trissy! We'll see her Saturday!" I say in a rush.

Jaclyn smiles again, her eyes back to something else on her screen, and says, "See ya," and ends the call.

One minute and forty-two seconds. My mom and I look at each other. "Well! That was short and sweet!" she says, getting up, stretching.

"Mom, are you sure about this?" I ask.

"Sure about what?" she asks. She's looking at her phone. "Oh wow, it's already here," she mutters to herself. "I'm just going to send this over to Stella to look at, but I'm sure it's fine."

Stella is a customer-turned-friend, and she's a lawyer.

"Mom!" I say, suddenly desperate for her attention.

She looks at me, startled.

"Are you sure about all this?" I ask, waving my arms around vaguely.

She looks confused. "Sure about what?"

"This weekend. This influencer stuff. Doesn't it feel a bit crazy?"

My mom exhales. "Some people thought I was crazy to become a single parent by choice. Other people thought I was crazy to open a coffee shop on my own. This is actually one of the least crazy things I've done."

28

That night I'm trying to work on my homework, but my phone keeps buzzing with notifications. Right after the call, my friends had texted me, wanting all the details of the phone call with Trissy, but I told them there wasn't much to report and gave them the rundown of talking to her assistant.

They kept asking more questions that I didn't have answers to (Amber wanted to know what Trissy was going to wear; Evie wanted to know if Trissy was going anywhere else in Briar Glen), and they seemed disappointed that I didn't have more to tell them.

Finally, I sent them a message saying I'd see them at school the next day, and then I go to bed, dreaming about meeting Trissy. But in the dreams I'm missing my tongue and I can't communicate with Trissy. I wake up, sweating.

🍂

The next few days pass in a weird blur of school, where everyone has to tell me their opinion about Trissy visiting; and hectic afternoons at the coffee shop, where we're busy with customers but also trying to clean, organize, and get the shop influencer-ready. Trissy messages a few times, letting us know she'll be at the shop Saturday morning at eight, and she doesn't want anyone else there. So I keep updating Cup o' Jo's Instagram, letting everyone know we'll be closed to the public for an hour, which some people think is cool. And some people think is ridiculous. I make signs about the closure for the shop, and I hear customers reading the signs, whispering to one another, shooting my mom and me sidelong glances. Sometimes I can tell when people think Trissy's visit is a good idea or a bad one, and other times I'm clue-less, which means I spend too much time analyzing every customer's facial expression, body language, even what they order.

Finally, it's Saturday morning. At 7:55 we still have a few cus-tomers milling about, including Mrs. Vervone, but my mom politely notifies them that we'll be closed to the public for just an hour. Some look offended; some look delighted. I hold the door open as everyone leaves. Mrs. Vervone whispers, "Good luck," to me.

At eight, my mom and I are standing behind the counter, ready. Or, as ready as we can be. The shop is the cleanest it's been in weeks, and we even put up some more Halloween decorations. I end up wearing my usual T-shirt and jeans, because my apron is covering my clothes, and also because every dress I tried on just looked wrong. My mom is in a white flowy blouse, black jean capris, and has a long headband scarf in her hair. She looks elegant and professional.

"You look beautiful, Mom."

"So do you." She gives my hands a squeeze, and I realize my hands are sweating.

We let go, and then the door to the coffee shop jingles open, and a teenage girl walks in. She's dressed flawlessly in a white sweater poncho, a tan hat, black leggings, and brown knee-high boots. Her blond hair is curled to perfection to her shoulders. Even so, despite her perfect appearance, it takes me a second to recognize her without hundreds of emojis swirling by her head, without any animated animal ears on her face or head, without any filters.

"Trissy!" I say, trying to recover. I feel both oddly starstruck and surprised by how . . . unfiltered she is. Almost, ordinary?

She smiles, her teeth white and perfect, and puts out her arms as she walks toward the counter. "Lucy!" she squeals as she gives me one of those loose hugs where we don't actually touch. "It is so amazing to meet you in person!"

She smells like a million amazing-smelling hair and makeup products at once, and it's all a little overwhelming.

She pulls away from me before I have time to say anything and turns to my mom. "And Joanna, or Ms. Kane—which would you prefer I call you?—it's such an honor to meet you in person! I love that this coffee shop is female operated, owned, and driven!" She puts out her hand to shake with my mom.

For one of the first times in my life, my mom looks a little flustered as she shakes Trissy's hand. "Oh, Joanna is fine! Thank you, Trissy, again for stopping by Briar Glen and Cup o' Jo. We're so happy you're here!"

"Oh my gosh, this town is so adorable! But before I get too far ahead of myself, and so I can save some content for the live stream, I'll just give you a quick rundown. I already met the Harper family across the street, so they know the plan, too. My team is outside ready to go, but I wanted to come in and say hi first."

"Your team, right," I say, trying to recover.

"We'll get some content of us meeting—I'll do the same at Java Junction—and then I'll try both of your delicious-looking pumpkin spice lattes, I'm thinking outside, with the mountain behind me, and soon we'll know which one is better!"

"Got it," I say, trying to keep up.

"Is it okay if I run to the bathroom, freshen up a bit?" my mom asks, still looking a little flustered.

"Of course! I'll do the same after you," Trissy says.

"Right, thanks," my mom says, and it strikes me as so odd that she's thanking a stranger for letting her use a bathroom in a coffee shop she owns, but everything about this is so odd.

"The 'story' you and your mom have is so adorable!" Trissy says as we hear the bathroom door close. She puts "story" into air quotes.

"What 'story'?" I ask, using my own air quotes right back.

She laughs, actually, no, she trills. Even in an empty coffee shop I realize she's performing. She looks quickly around her, seems to remember we're alone. "The 'story'"—again with the air quotes—"of you and your mom being so close, getting along so well."

I frown. "It's not a 'story'?" My fingers and brain are starting to cramp from all the air quotes.

She laughs again. "Sweetie, drop the act. My mother drives me nuts! The arguments we've had about me being an 'influencer,' about my clothes, about my 'image,' about my 'future.'" I speculate that she must have carpal tunnel from all her air quotes. "Sometimes I wonder why the neighbors haven't called the police for how loudly we've yelled at each other, the arguments we've had!" She laughs even louder, harder now, but stops when she realizes I'm not, that I'm just staring at her blankly.

"Oh, I mean we definitely get on each other's nerves!" I say quickly, trying to fill the space. "She reminds me a lot to chew with my mouth closed, that I can't put wet towels into the hamper . . ." Trissy looks at me, eagerly waiting for me to go on. But I can't. I won't. My mom and I don't have a perfect relationship. But does anyone have a perfect relationship with their parents? When I was younger, I used to get really upset that she was working so hard, I had babysitters, she couldn't take me to the playground whenever I wanted, she was always tired, our family was different because it was just the two of us. But I don't want to—need to—tell any of this to Trissy. "It's . . . hard being a teenage girl sometimes," I finish awkwardly, vaguely.

Trissy narrows her eyes at me for just a second, then smiles brightly, back to performing, even though we're still alone in the shop except for my mom. We hear the door to the bathroom open, and Trissy quickly and quietly says, "That Jack Harper is something, too!"

But she walks away before I can ask her what she means, if he's a good something or a bad something.

She's in the bathroom for a while, and my mom asks me, "You ready?"

I shrug. "No?"

She laughs, gives me a little hug. "Well, that makes two of us!"

Trissy reappears, looking just as flawless as before. "Okay, so I'll go across the street, make my introductions at Java Junction, get some quick footage of the interior and of the Harpers. We'll do the same here, quick shots of the interior and of you guys, and then, Lucy, do you mind carrying the drink outside?"

She looks around the shop, a brief look of horror crossing her face. "The drink is already made, right?"

"Yes! Right here!" I say, pulling it from the hot plate where it's been staying warm.

"Lovely!" she practically sings. "Anyway, you can carry your PSL, Jack will carry his, and soon all my fans will know who has the better pumpkin spice latte!"

She makes it sound so simple, so easy. "We good?" she asks my mom and me.

"We're good," my mom says, and I think I nod.

She walks out, leaving behind the smell of hair products.

My mom and I watch Trissy walk into Java Junction, her phone in hand. I see Jack laughing with her, the obvious ease he has in front of the camera. His parents are laughing and talking with her, and I give my mom a quick look. "We can do this, right?" I think my voice is shaking.

"Honey, we can do anything," my mom says, squeezing my shoulders.

"Right, we can do anything," I echo weakly.

29

Before I know it, Trissy walks into Cup o' Jo, her phone on selfie mode. "And here I am at Cup o' Jo, owned by local mother slash daughter team Joanna and Lucy." She pushes a button, and I know she's recording us, but I freeze, suddenly forgetting how to make my mouth form words.

"It's so nice to meet you, ladies!" Trissy says.

I don't know if she's back on selfie mode or what she's doing or where I'm supposed to look, but my mom says, "It's our pleasure to have you here, Trissy."

"So in contrast to the giant coffee chain across the street, here we have quaint. Local. Locally sourced ingredients. You won't find anything mass-produced here, right, ladies?"

I nod, and my mom says, "That's right. We create all our own drinks, make all the desserts you see here." She gestures to our pastry case, and I think Trissy is getting footage of what my mom is showing her, but I have no way of knowing.

"And on to the reason we're here, the star of the show, the pumpkin spice latte," Trissy cuts in. She looks at me, her phone pointed at me, and my mom gives me a slight nudge with her elbow, and I pull out the pumpkin spice latte.

Trissy walks over to me, her phone trained on the drink, and I feel like the pumpkin spice latte in my hands is some kind of rare animal, and it strikes me again how ridiculous this all is.

"And I understand that you created this drink yourself, Lucy?" Trissy asks me.

"I did, yeah. I mean with some help from a . . . friend," I say.

"Oooh, sounds like there is more to that story!" Trissy says with a wink.

I must look scared because she quickly says, "But we'll hear about that some other time." And then she's back on selfie mode, walking out of Cup o' Jo, and I walk behind her, carrying the precious drink.

At the same time the door to Java Junction opens, and Jack is carrying his own precious rare animal. Our eyes meet, and he gives me another one of those smiles, and I feel a little less nervous, even though it's his fault I'm nervous at all, his fault this whole challenge exists, his fault we're in this ridiculous situation.

"Gosh, can we just take another look around beautiful Briar Glen! Can you believe this place?" Trissy asks. She slowly spins her phone around, showing all her live viewers Briar Glen's Main

Street in the fall. I hear and see the likes, the hearts, and despite myself I can't help but feel pride.

She switches back to selfie mode. "Right? Can you think of a more perfect place for a pumpkin spice latte challenge? Okay, guys, give me the goods," she says. I realize she's talking to Jack and me, and I don't know who is supposed to hand over their drink first, but then Jack and his family quickly cross the street. Trissy turns her phone to Jack, and he gives a theatrical bow before handing her the drink.

"So here we have the Java Junction pumpkin spice latte, the classic pumpkin latte, the pumpkin spice latte that really started the craze of the pumpkin spice latte! A latte we all know and love." She is back on selfie mode as she takes a sip.

She closes her eyes, savoring the drink, swallows slowly. "I mean, does it get more perfectly fall than this drink? I don't think so!"

I have a horrible feeling in my stomach, like when I lost the fall festival dessert contest. Is Trissy here just to humiliate me? To make Cup o' Jo look bad?

She looks back into her phone again. "However, if anyone can make a better pumpkin spice latte than Java Junction, I have a feeling it's going to be Cup o' Jo. I'm ready!" she says.

I realize that's my cue, so I take a step forward, handing Trissy my drink.

She makes a big show of inhaling the drink. "Wow, guys, I wish you could smell how good this smells." She inhales again. "If this tastes half as good as it smells, I'm in for a treat," she says.

"Okay, here goes nothing." She pauses dramatically, and then takes a sip of my pumpkin spice latte.

She closes her eyes again, savoring my drink this time. And then, nothing. She just sits there with her eyes closed, not saying a word.

I look at my mom in a panic and she just shrugs. I look at Jack, and he shrugs, too.

Then Trissy's eyes pop open. "Oh my gosh, so sorry, you guys. I was having a moment. Now *that* is a pumpkin spice latte."

And then she takes another slow sip, and another. "Wow," she finally says. She shakes her head. "All right, you guys, you ready to hear the winner?" she asks, peering into the phone.

I see and hear hearts and thumbs-up emojis filling her screen.

"The winner of the Briar Glen pumpkin spice latte contest? It's . . ." She pauses dramatically, looking first at me, then at Jack. "It's Cup o' Jo!"

I see and hear more hearts and thumbs-up on her screen, and then realize Trissy is pointing her phone at my mom and me, and this is the part where I'm supposed to do something. Except I suddenly can't say or do anything.

My mom is talking, though, saying something about what an honor it is to have Trissy in Briar Glen, what an honor it is that she liked Cup o' Jo's pumpkin spice latte so much, that she knows how good Java Junction's pumpkin spice latte is.

And Trissy is saying something back, and then she's turning her phone on silent, putting it in her pocket.

And then it's over. Everything feels so quiet now that Trissy's phone is away. "Guys, for real, this drink is amazing," she says to my mom and me.

"Thank you so much. But it's all Lucy," my mom says proudly.

Jack and his parents are laughing, talking about something, and I quickly say, "Like I said, I got a lot of help and advice from a friend."

Jack looks up at me and winks.

Trissy has already moved on, though, and she has her phone back out and is taking selfies with my pumpkin spice latte. "I think I'm going to walk around, get some pictures of your adorable town," she says without looking away from her phone, so I'm not sure who she's talking to.

I'm not sure if she knows who she is talking to, either.

My mom turns to Jack's parents. "Thanks for being willing to do that!" she says.

"We should be thanking you, and bowing down to your pumpkin spice latte," Jack's mom says, laughing.

"Hey, congrats, seriously, though," Jack's dad says, shaking my mom's hand, then mine.

It's kind of weird to shake his hand, but I do and say, "Thank you. And really, I couldn't have done it without Jack's help and advice."

"Lucy, give yourself some credit! The syrup blend was all you," Jack says. "All I did was tell you to take your time bringing things together. I didn't know what I was talking about! I gave you some vague advice and you went with it."

"Vague advice? You told me I was bringing the flavors together too soon."

"I didn't, actually. I just blabbered on about trying to unite things too soon and you took that and ran with it."

"So you didn't know what you were talking about?" I ask.

"Not a clue," he says.

"Jack Harper—" I start.

But I realize I'm not mad at him. How could I be?

"It was all you, Lucy," he says.

I look at his parents, at my mom, back at Jack, and they're all smiling at me.

But why can't I smile back at them? Why am I not happier we won the pumpkin spice latte challenge?

"I think I need some water," I say, and go back into Cup o' Jo in a daze.

My mom follows me in. "You okay, honey?"

I nod. "I think so? I don't know. I thought I'd feel happier that we won," I admit. "I just feel kinda . . . blank?"

"Well, it makes sense. It was a really intense few days and a lot of buildup, and now it's done. It's like the day-after-Christmas feeling. Or after a really busy day at the shop. It's a lot of adrenaline, and then your body needs time to recover."

"I guess," I say, unconvinced.

"Let me get you some water," my mom says.

While she's up, I start reading through some of the notifications on my phone, including my friends' texts.

Amber

> OMG CONGRATS!

Evie

> I mean, duh? That latte is really, really good, Lucy.

Amber

> Trissy is at Betsy's Ice Cream Barn. You guys should check it out.

Evie

> Also need to check out Cup o' Jo's account. You guys are blowing up.

But I don't want to check Trissy's social media. I don't want to check Cup o' Jo's social media. I just want the world to be quiet for a second.

My mom puts the glass of water in front of me. "It's okay to feel overwhelmed. This is a lot to take in."

I nod, still dazed. I hear the front-door bell jingle and look up. Customers, of course. And they all have their phones out, taking a million pictures of themselves, of one another. Some of them, like Dawn Lucas, another one of my mom's friends, are even taking videos.

My mom says, "Take the afternoon off, okay? We've got Sheva and Danielle and Will. We'll be okay."

"Are you sure?" I ask. "I can still work." But even as the words leave my mouth, I know they're a lie. I can't stand behind the counter and smile at customers. I can't make another pumpkin spice latte.

I stand up to leave, and Dawn says, "Lucy! Can I get a picture with you?"

"With me?" I ask, confused.

"Yeah!" she says. "I mean, only if you want. If it's okay with your mom?"

"No, it's fine," I say.

Dawn stands close to me, smiling with a thumb up,

and I try to paste a smile on my face, not sure if I'm successful.

"Thank you so much!" she says.

"Um, you're welcome."

I give one last look to my mom, who makes a shooing motion with her hands, and I head out of Cup o' Jo.

On the walk home, I run into some kids from my high school, Megan Merrell and Tasha Lewis. "Hey, congrats, Lucy!" they say in unison.

"Thanks," I say, but it's like I'm listening to someone else talk, hearing someone else's voice.

My name is being called, and I don't want to turn around. I don't want to talk to anyone else or have my picture taken. But it's Jack's voice. It's *Jack*.

I turn around, and he jogs to catch up with me.

"You okay?" he asks.

I sigh. "Yes? No? I don't know."

"The challenge thing was weird, right?"

"Totally weird," I say. "I thought I'd be more excited that we won. But I worry that we won for the wrong reasons? Like we're trying to please other people? Like we're trying so hard to make other people happy, and we're trying to turn Cup o' Jo into something we're not?" I don't realize the words are true until they're out of my mouth.

Jack is quiet, thinking about what I said. "I guess I don't see it that way?" he finally says.

"Really? How do you see it?"

"I see it as you wanting to do anything and everything you can to make sure your mom's shop is financially stable. I see it as an act of love."

I wrinkle my nose. "You don't think that's a bit dramatic?"

"You know what's dramatic?"

"What?" I ask, curious.

"This!" he says, showing me his phone, all the people who have commented on Trissy's post.

"Wow," I whisper.

"Right?" he says. "People are getting this dramatic, this excited about coffee. Just let that sink in for a second. Coffee. Not oxygen. Not space travel. Coffee."

"I see what you mean," I admit.

"Anyway, it seems silly. That a drink can create so much . . ."

"Drama?" I offer.

"I was going to say happiness," Jack says. "I was going to say your drink brings lots of people happiness. And who are we to judge them for that?"

"Yeah, I understand."

"What you need to find is what brings *you* happiness," he says.

"Me?" I repeat.

"Yes, you."

"Helping my mom out makes me happy—"

"Outside of Cup o' Jo," he says. "What brings Lucy, the teenager who works at Cup o' Jo—not Lucy, the Cup o' Jo employee and that's her only form of identity—happiness."

"Baking," I say without a second thought. "I miss it. I love it."

"Are you talking about baking for Cup o' Jo?" he asks.

"Well, I do love that part. But I also love baking. For me. My mom and I used to bake together all the time when I was a kid. I loved it. I still do. I love listening to her while she tells me stories about when she was little, baking with my grandma. I love creating recipes, mastering recipes." I pause, thinking. "And, I have to admit, it was pretty fun helping you with that pumpkin pie."

He scoffs. "Helping me? You mean teaching me basic baking concepts?"

I laugh. "Yeah, something like that."

"Well, there's your answer, then," Jack says.

"I need to bake more for myself?" I ask, confused. "Bake for others? But I already do that at Cup o' Jo."

"Bring together two small separate ideas for one big idea."

I groan. "I'm having a flashback to when you gave me advice about how to make the perfect pumpkin spice latte."

"And look how quickly you figured out that totally vague advice."

I'm thinking about his words. "I should bake for other people? But not at Cup o' Jo?"

He looks at me, his green eyes twinkling. "I think the rest is for you to figure out."

"Have you and Amber and Evie been talking?"

"No?" He looks amused. "Why?"

"Nothing! You guys just have a penchant for dropping vague advice and words of encouragement on me."

"You say that like it's a bad thing."

We've made it to my house now. "Want to try your hand at making another pumpkin spice latte?" I ask.

Jack looks horrified for a second, then quickly recovers. "Hilarious."

I grin. "I know."

"It was fun, though," he says.

"What was?"

"Making the drink. All our attempts."

"I don't know if I'd call that clove coffee fun," I say.

"Fair enough," he says, laughing.

"We could do it again sometime? I mean, not the pumpkin spice lattes. But I could give you more baking lessons, maybe?"

Jack smiles. "I'd like that."

"Me too."

He looks like he wants to say more, but finally he just says, "I should get back to the shop. My parents are probably wondering where I am."

"Okay."

We stand there, just looking at each other.

"And, oh, congrats on winning the contest! Where are my manners?" Jack says. He puts out his hand, like we're going to shake hands, and I just look at his hand, then at him.

"A handshake? For real?"

"Too much?" he asks.

"Way."

"How about a hug, then?" he asks.

In response, I reach out my arms and wrap them around him.

He seems surprised but quickly relaxes into the hug. "I think I'm supposed to hug *you*, as, like, a congratulations?" he says. His words tickle against my ear.

"Shut up," I say.

"Okay," he says.

And we hug. For a long time.

I finally pull away. "You should get back."

"Right," he says.

"See you soon?"

"See you soon."

I watch the definitely-not-a-robot Jack Harper walk down my street.

I let myself inside my house, scoop up Pancakes, and text my friends.

Lucy

I think I need another emergency baking session.

Amber

Say no more.

Evie

On my way.

When Evie arrives a few minutes later, she looks confused as I open the door. "This is like a celebratory baking session, right? Like a good emergency, not a bad one? Should I have gotten a bottle of sparkling apple cider?"

"I'm not sure," I say honestly.

She follows me into the kitchen and says, "I'm sorry, but why aren't you jumping up and down right now?"

I laugh. "I think it's an internal jumping up and down?"

Evie waits for me to say more, but the doorbell is ringing. I let Amber in, and she squeals, "Oh my god, you guys did it! I mean, I knew that you would, of course, but eeek!" She starts jumping up and down in the entryway.

Evie comes out of the kitchen. "We're not doing the whole jumping up and down thing," she says.

"We're not?" Amber abruptly stops jumping, panting.

"Just follow me into the kitchen," I say.

My friends gather around my kitchen island, looking at me curiously.

I realize I don't know what to say.

"So can we jump up and down more?" Amber asks, breaking the silence.

I laugh. "Okay. Yes. We can jump up and down. I'll even allow some squealing."

So we all jump up and down, and there is even some squealing, though I see the confusion on my friends' faces.

"Well, that was weird and slightly awkward and felt totally fake," Evie says.

"And I still want to know why we're here for an emergency baking session?" Amber persists.

"I think I've been losing myself in Cup o' Jo too much," I blurt out.

My friends look at me in shocked silence.

"I know, you guys have been telling me that for weeks. My mom has been telling me that for weeks. But I think it finally hit me today when Trissy was here. When I realized I wasn't more excited about winning. I think I'm ready to be a teenager?"

Evie and Amber shoot each other concerned looks. "This is a good thing!" I say. "Now we can jump up and down."

And we do, and it feels much better than the jumping up and down we just did to celebrate winning Trissy's contest. So much better.

"You're right, Amber. I'm going to make a celebratory dessert. Not an emergency one."

"To celebrate Trissy choosing your drink?" Amber asks.

"No. To celebrate me being a teenager," I say. "Homemade brownies coming right up. And I'm not putting a second of it on Cup o' Jo's social media account."

We don't talk about Cup o' Jo or Trissy or even Java Junction or Jack the rest of the afternoon. By the time my mom comes home, I feel the most relaxed and happiest I've felt in a long time.

"The whole gang is here!" she says.

I still see that spark of excitement in her eyes that I saw earlier in the day.

"You trying out new recipes for Cup o' Jo?" she asks, looking around the messy kitchen.

"No, actually," I say. "I just felt like making brownies."

Now her smile is even bigger. "I'm so happy to hear that! You guys want to stay for dinner? I'll order pizza?"

And she does, and it's the most normal night to cap off the most unusual day of my life.

When Evie and Amber leave, my mom is stacking plates in the dishwasher.

"I'm sorry about today, Mom," I say.

She looks confused. "Sorry? About what?" she asks.

"That I left. That I couldn't stick around and help," I say. "I was feeling so overwhelmed."

"Honey, I'd be worried if you didn't feel overwhelmed," my mom says. "I'm so proud of you for making that drink, for all the work you've done at the shop, but I really think it's time for you—"

"I think I need to do more for myself," I interrupt.

My mom looks surprised for a second, but then she says, "Go on. I want to hear about this."

"I know everyone, including you, wants me to do things besides Cup o' Jo. Have a life outside Cup o' Jo. But I don't think people understand that Cup o' Jo is my life. But it also inspires my life.

Or my life is inspired by Cup o' Jo?" Suddenly it all seems too confusing to explain.

"I understand," my mom says. "Sometimes it can be hard to separate the two."

"Like, the baking. It's related to Cup o' Jo, yeah, but it's not the only reason I bake. I bake because I enjoy it. Because of the memories I have with you. Because that's what I grew up doing. And I like baking for my friends. And like when I showed Jack how to bake, it was fun?" I pause, something occurring to me. "Maybe I could go to culinary school?"

"You could—"

"But I also know I don't need to figure it all out right this second, either."

My mom says gently, "Exactly. If you're too busy planning your life, you're going to miss it. It's going to pass right by you."

"And I shouldn't be afraid to ask where the bathroom is, either," I say.

"What?" My mom gives me a confused look.

"Nothing. Long story," I say.

"Lucy, I'm so proud of you for making the pumpkin spice latte that you did, for all the work you've put into getting Cup o' Jo back on social media. But I want you to do things for you, Lucy. Lucy Kane. Not Lucy the employee of Cup o' Jo."

"I think I'm ready for that, too, Mom," I say.

She gives me a hug, and she smells like the coffee shop and pumpkin spice lattes. And I finally realize how good a pumpkin spice latte actually smells.

30

My mom tells me to take Sunday off from the coffee shop, and for once I don't argue. I hear her leave early in the morning, and I let myself sleep in. When I finally wake up, it's after ten.

I go to the kitchen, find some cereal, and start scrolling through my phone, checking Cup o' Jo's social media. We have more followers and even more people tagging us, posting pictures of my pumpkin spice latte, and there are pictures of Trissy all over Briar Glen.

But I put my phone down and enjoy my cereal in silence.

After breakfast, I pull out a stack of cookbooks, carefully turning the pages, running my finger over the penciled notes that are written in both my grandmother's neat cursive and my mom's chicken scratch.

Sub honey for maple syrup.

Dark brown sugar, not light brown.

Made this for Lucy's seventh bday—kids loved.

I smile, remembering my seventh birthday, the cake that my mom made from scratch: seven layers, each layer a different color of the rainbow.

A recipe for chocolate chip cookies: *Made with Lucy today. She did great following my directions!* There's a date in the corner. I was nine.

I dig through more cookbooks, find the recipe that I used as a starting point for my pumpkin pie, read all the notes, now in my own handwriting. Reading the recipe makes me think of when I taught Jack how to make a pumpkin pie, and I'm smiling even more now. I think about him measuring cream, then singing to it, how clueless he was at first about anything baking.

And then, an idea occurs to me. Baking is second nature to me, but it isn't for a lot of people. But what if I could make it easier for others, somehow? I mentioned culinary school to my mom, but that's a million years away. What if I could give lessons or tips now?

I think about all the followers Cup o' Jo has, how many people I could help, and then I start planning.

A little later, I position my phone on the counter, propped up against an old cookbook, sigh, and hit the record button. I wave to the camera and start talking.

"Um, hi, this is Lucy," I begin. "I'm um, Joanna's daughter. She owns and runs Cup o' Jo. Today I'm going to show you, or tell you, I guess, how to make apple chips." Then I smack myself in the forehead. Apple crisp. I sigh, hit record, and start again, but quickly stop when I trip over my own mom's name.

I get some water, do a lap around the house, look at myself in the mirror. "You can do this, Lucy."

This time, when I hit the record button, I'm ready. I still trip over a few words here and there as I introduce myself, but I say, "Can you tell this is my first time doing this?" and smile into my phone's camera. By the time I'm saying, "Today I'm going to show you how I make my version of apple crisp," I've almost forgotten I'm recording myself. Because I'm thinking back to all the times I've made the dessert with my mom throughout my life, all the apple crisp we've sold at the shop through the years, and thinking about and talking about baking sometimes feels as natural to me as breathing.

I stop recording when the apple crisp is in the oven, watch what I've captured so far, and it's not terrible.

I get a few more quick videos of myself taking the apple crisp out of the oven. I capture a quick video of myself eating the apple crisp, and then another because I feel weird talking with my mouth full, and eventually I get something I feel comfortable with.

I look through the videos, and I'm able to edit it all together into something close to decent. It definitely won't win any film awards, but it'll do. I post the video.

And I feel good.

31

The weather on Halloween night is beautiful. A little chill in the air, but not too cold. Clear sky, full of twinkling stars. Something about it reminds me of that Halloween I told Jack about. That perfect Halloween when I was five and my mom made my awesome witch costume, and everything just felt perfect. A night full of possibilities.

Cup o' Jo stops serving coffee at five o'clock, but as soon as the coffee goes away, my mom and I pull the bowls of candy out.

We get the littlest trick-or-treaters first. The ones either strapped to their parents' chests in baby carriers or being pushed in strollers or toddling in on feet that aren't quite steady yet. A lot of them are dressed in fuzzy costumes, like elephants and squirrels, and characters from TV shows I used to watch when I was a kid.

A lot of them seem confused by my mom's black cat costume and my pumpkin costume, and a lot of them don't understand trick-or-treating or what they're supposed to do, which makes the whole thing that much more adorable. Some of the parents seem to feel guilty about taking candy since their trick-or-treaters are so young, but my mom and I tell them to enjoy, like we do every year.

Some of the elementary-age kids start coming in, and I hear one say to her friend, "Trissy was here, remember?"

Her friend is focused on the bowl of candy on our counter and doesn't care, though.

It's Halloween, and this is Cup o' Jo, my home away from home, and no matter who comes in here or what they order, no one can take that away from me.

We watch the group leave, and my mom puts her arm around my shoulders. "I swear you were just that small last month," she says, giving me a squeeze.

"I thought it was last week?" I tease.

"Maybe it was five minutes ago," she says, laughing. "But I'm so proud of who that little girl has become. Is becoming."

"Mom, don't start with the mushy stuff. It'll make my makeup run!" I say, pointing to my eyes, which I've added green mascara to. But I'm laughing, too.

We're both still laughing when the door opens and Jack walks in. I stop laughing abruptly, and then I'm laughing even harder than I was before. Because Jack has made himself into a Pieface for Halloween. I don't know how he did it, but he's got pieces of pie stuck all over his face and is dressed all in brown, like a pecan pie.

"It's a little hard to talk with all this glue on my face," he says, not moving his mouth much.

"You win," I say, doubling over. "You win!"

Jack bows carefully, one hand holding on to the pie stuck to his face. I realize he's got something in his other hand. A small sign.

He stands up from his bow, and I ask him, "What's with the sign?"

"It's for you," he says, handing it to me. "It's for your front door."

I look down at the sign in my hand. *VOTED BEST PUMPKIN SPICE LATTE IN BRIAR GLEN.*

I look up, and he's smiling at me. "Thank you," I say. I want to say more, so much more, but Evie and Amber walk in behind Jack, and when he faces them, they start laughing, too.

I turn to my mom. "I'm going to go out with my friends. We're just going to walk around, look at costumes, hang out for a bit," I say, before she has a chance to tell me to. Before she has a chance to remind me to be a teenager.

"Good!" everyone says at once.

I hang up my Cup o' Jo apron and give my mom one more hug.

It's just gotten dark outside, and I gently grab Jack's face, looking at it in a streetlight. He really did do an amazing job with his costume.

"The original Pieface was much better," Jack says. He touches my hand on his face.

"I'm not so sure about that," I say. "I like this version a lot, too. A whole lot."

I walk off into the cool night air with my friends. I'm not sure where we're going yet.

But that's okay.

ACKNOWLEDGMENTS

I wrote this book while undergoing some really scary medical stuff, and this book served as such a warm, pleasant escape. I want to thank everyone at Memorial Sloan Kettering Cancer Center, especially my treatment team, Dr. Rui Wang, Katie Rudy-Tomczak, and Jen Keller. *Thank you* doesn't seem adequate enough for the life-saving treatment you gave me, not to mention the emotional comfort, love, and encouragement. Thank you also to Dr. Monica Morrow, Dr. Colleen McCarthy, Dr. Vance Andrew Broach, Dr. Megan Lillian Gilman, and to all the other doctors, nurses, technicians, and office staff I met throughout my various office visits and hospital stays. A special thank-you to all my infusion nurses as well—I wish I could give you all a million warm blankets.

Thank you to my mom, Greg, and Erin for the visits and the care and the mashed potatoes. Thank you to Nick and Mila for keeping me brave and making me feel strong. Thank you to Dawn and Bob, Natalie, Roman and Robin, Victor, Katia and Mary, Francesca and Alex, Zenon and Summer, the Casads, Mary Jo, Kevin, Gene and Susan, Chris and Amal, Gina, Cosmo, Lisa, Loren, Nicole, Whitneigh, and Mary for being my loving family. Thank you to the O'Briens, the Kolbs, and the Lachers for being my loving family, too.

Thank you to Jessie, Stephanie, Beth and Charlie, and Heather for the transportation at all hours. Thank you to Oriane, Laura, Stella, Lucky, Rudha, Doug, Linda, Shasta, Marianne, Colm, Mona, Carolyn, Katie, Rebecca, Rachel Losh, Rachel Parekh De Azua, Lauren O'Neill Butler, Lauren Biggs, Nathan, Chad, Kristen, Megan, Raquel, Lavina, Caitlin, Molly, Nico, Billy, Elizabeth, Jen, Jenn, Kellie, Lindsey, Sarah, Kristal, Angela, Autumn, Tricia, Debbie, Alison, Diane, Christy, Amy, Pearl, Lisa, Frisco, Quinn, Amanda, Joena, and Anna for the texts, the emails, the cards, the phone calls, the walks, the talks, the care packages, and the love.

An extra-large pumpkin spice latte to Mary for all those Wednesdays you took care of Mila, and to Liz, for treating Mila like your own daughter.

Thank you to Cathryn Biordi, Jane Cervone, Diana Fernandez, Trish Silverman, Betsy Purdy, Dawn Hammond, Donna Consaga, Angela Zappala, Camille Cortina, Meg Calvert-Cason,

Don Schiller, and Kim Asch, for ensuring that my daughter was in excellent hands at school.

Thank you to Devon Burns, Sarah Crow, Ryan Biracree, and Emily Hare for the macaroni and cheese train, and thank you to everyone else who brought us food (there really are too many of you to list!), especially Caiming Cheung, Elise Derevjanik, Jennifer Meister, and Sparrow's Nest.

As always, Scholastic has been a dream to work with. Orlando Dos Reis, thank you for your insightful edits, for brainstorming with me, for all our conversations about pumpkin-flavored everything, and for never doubting that I'd be able to write this book. Thank you to Stephanie Yang for the book and cover design, and thank you to Leni Kauffman for beautifully capturing Lucy and Jack just as they had appeared in my own head. Thank you to Cindy Durand, Janell Harris, Claire Flanagan, Catherine Weening, and Cady Zeng for your sharp eyes. Thank you to the production department, and the marketing, sales, and publicity departments, for all you do to get my books into readers' hands.

Thank you to my local bookstore, Stanza, and thank you to all booksellers and librarians for your vital work.

And finally, I have to thank Beacon, my beautiful city, my very own Briar Glen.

ABOUT THE AUTHOR

Katie Cicatelli-Kuc is the author of two other young adult novels and an assorted collection of books for young readers. She lives in a town not unlike Briar Glen in New York's Hudson Valley with her family and her animals. Katie loves anything and everything fall, including pumpkin spice lattes, even when they're made with artificial ingredients.

Follow her on Instagram at @katie_cicatelli_writes.